SPECIAL MESSAGE TO READERS

THE ULVERSCROFT FOUNDATION
(registered UK charity number 264873)
was established in 1972 to provide funds for
research, diagnosis and treatment of eye diseases.
Examples of major projects funded by
the Ulverscroft Foundation are:-

- The Children's Eye Unit at Moorfields Eye Hospital, London
- The Ulverscroft Children's Eye Unit at Great Ormond Street Hospital for Sick Children
- Funding research into eye diseases and treatment at the Department of Ophthalmology, University of Leicester
- The Ulverscroft Vision Research Group, Institute of Child Health
- Twin operating theatres at the Western Ophthalmic Hospital, London
- The Chair of Ophthalmology at the Royal Australian College of Ophthalmologists

You can help further the work of the Foundation
by making a donation or leaving a legacy.
Every contribution is gratefully received. If you
would like to help support the Foundation or
require further information, please contact:

THE ULVERSCROFT FOUNDATION
The Green, Bradgate Road, Anstey
Leicester LE7 7FU, England
Tel: (0116) 236 4325
website: www.foundation.ulverscroft.com

JESSICA'S DEATH

Detectives Jilly Garvey and Dan Lee are no strangers to violent death. Nevertheless, the brutal killing of an affluent woman, whose body is found in a decaying urban neighborhood miles from her home, impacts them deeply. Their investigative abilities are stretched to the limit as clues don't add up and none of the possible suspects seem quite right. As they dig deeper into the background of the victim, a portrait emerges of a profoundly troubled woman. Will they find the answers they need to bring a vicious killer to justice?

TONY GLEESON

JESSICA'S DEATH

Complete and Unabridged

LINFORD
Leicester

First published in Great Britain

First Linford Edition
published 2017

A catalogue record for this book is available
from the British Library.

ISBN 978–1–4448–3239–6

Published by
F. A. Thorpe (Publishing)
Anstey, Leicestershire

Set by Words & Graphics Ltd.
Anstey, Leicestershire
Printed and bound in Great Britain by
T. J. International Ltd., Padstow, Cornwall

This book is printed on acid-free paper

1

'Mondays stink' is a common sentiment, but for Delino Washington, Mondays *literally* stank. So did Tuesdays, Wednesdays, Thursdays and Fridays. But Mondays were the worst.

All things considered, Delino didn't really mind his job with the city's Department of Public Works. He took home a decent paycheck and the benefits were good, especially the medical and dental, which meant something for a man with a family. He hadn't experienced a breakdown in some time, due to the recent upgrade of their trucks. Even his fellow sanitation workers were, for the most part, reasonable enough people. He had very few complaints. Being one of the guys who collect the city's garbage could have been a lot worse.

If only he had a different route.

The neighborhood at five in the morning looked lethargic and empty. Traffic, with the exception of his rumbling DPW vehicle, was nonexistent. The dawning light was casting an orange tinge over the quiet emptiness of short, narrow Tustin Street. It might have been peaceful and pretty; to Delino, it was still depressing. Large wheeled bins of plastic — green and black — were lined up along the curbs awaiting the claws of his bright blue truck to reach out like some metal bird of prey, scoop them up one by one and dump their contents into eagerly opening maws.

The locale was known locally as Sheffield, named after the main drag only a block away. The whole neighborhood was festering; that was the perfect word for it, Delino decided as he navigated his truck around parked cars. The garbage actually stank worse here than in other neighborhoods. On other routes, people were reasonably careful about how they put out their refuse. Here, nobody really cared. They just dumped stuff on the streets. The buildings on this block, owned by absentee slumlords, were neglected and degenerating: peeling paint, broken windows. The people were rotting. It was a drug neighborhood, deserted by day and dangerous at night, populated almost entirely by people who had given up on the promise of life.

Delino had been born in a bombed-out neighborhood only a couple of degrees better than this one. His father and mother, struggling against the onset of despair, had dragged their family out of it by intelligence, unflagging energy, and a sense of mission. Delino's current family had never needed to experience this kind of thing. They lived in a nice house in a nice part of the city. The kids attended good schools. He did not want his kids to know about places like this. He did not even like driving through them himself. That was the one downside of his job: he wished he had a different route.

He braked the truck next to a large black garbage container and worked the lever that extended the lifting arm out to it. As the arm began to hoist its load, he felt definite resistance from the bin. He had done this long enough to gauge the weight. There was something heavy in this one. Sometimes they dumped stupid junk into the bin, like stolen or broken appliances, even bricks or cinder blocks, only God knew why. The minds of drug addicts, Delino considered.

One of these days, who knew, he might find ...

He looked out the window at the arm raising the bin. He caught a glimpse of what was sticking out of the top of the black container.

He yanked the lever and brought the arm back down, slapping the bin to the pavement with a loud *slam*. Then he just sat there in the cab for a long time. He was really hoping his eyes had been playing tricks on him.

That *thing* he always feared might happen ... had it just happened?

He finally opened the door of the cab and stepped down into the street. He didn't want to look. He was afraid of what he was going to find.

It was exactly what he dreaded, just what he worried might someday happen here in this lousy section of town.

⋆   ⋆   ⋆

By seven a.m., tiny Tustin Street contained more people than it ordinarily might have in the space of an entire day. Its one-block

4

stretch had been cordoned off with police vehicles and layers of bright yellow tape proclaiming POLICE LINE DO NOT CROSS in heavy black capital letters. Uniformed officers, jump-suited Scientific Investigation Division technicians, and white-coated medical examiners moved purposefully about, working in well-practiced choreography around one another. The blue sanitation truck remained parked at a nearby curb; its driver, Delino Washington, sat at the same curb, conversing with a standing patrol officer.

One focus of the activity was a large black plastic garbage container which had been overturned, its contents carefully distributed over the nearby pavement. Two investigators were processing the bin and the various detritus on the ground. Nearby on the pavement lay the second focus of attention, partly covered by a heavy white tarpaulin.

It's hard to mistake a human body — in this case a very dead one.

Detectives Jilly Garvey and Dan Lee, who had just arrived, stood over the body, staring down at it. A heavyset man in a white coat had been squatting down beside the body, making notes on a clipboard, and now rose to greet them.

'Well, Detectives, good to see you.' He didn't say it, he delivered it, in the tone of an ironic joke. That was Mickey Kendrick's way, Jilly knew. The veteran ME's droopy bloodhound scowl and deadpan monotone belied a sharp, incisive professional mind. It took a while to get used to Mickey but Jilly was always glad to see him on one of their cases. Very little ever got by him. He prided himself on being quick but thorough and efficient.

'So what have we got here, Mickey?' she asked.

'She took a good beating. The evidence is consistent with some kind of hard blunt object, and likely fists as well. Broken ribs, skull fracture, broken nose, bruising all over. Some of the bruises seem post-mortem, indicating rage. The attacker didn't stop once she was dead.' He nodded his chin toward the container. 'Then she got stuffed into that trash bin.'

Dan looked pale and solemn. Some things weren't getting any easier, even though he was no longer the rookie detective in the unit. Jilly tried to ignore the uneasiness in her own stomach, feeling the responsibility as the senior partner.

Mickey looked back and forth at them. 'I'm pretty much through with my examination here, if you'd like to give her a look.'

Jilly had already snapped on one of the pairs of disposable plastic gloves she carried in her pocket. She knelt down beside the body, carefully pulling back the tarp to fully expose it. 'Thanks, Mickey.'

'Doesn't seem to be any ID. I'd guess she's in her forties. I'm estimating time of death at around eleven last night. When you're ready, we'll take her. I ought to be able to get to a more extensive examination back at the lab by tomorrow. You're lucky. No gridlock to speak of right now.'

'That would be most appreciated,' Jilly replied a bit absently as she began to sweep her gaze over the body of the woman lying supine on the ground in front of her.

'Besides, looking at what he did to her, I'd think you'd want to make this guy a priority.'

Jilly nodded grimly. 'If it is a guy.'

'Oh, it's a guy. Whoever did this was *very* strong and didn't hold back. He was tall, judging from the directionality of some of the blows. You're looking for a big hulk of a guy. Count on it.' Mickey tipped his hat to them and turned away.

Dan had pulled on his own pair of gloves and had squatted down across the body from Jilly, a notebook in hand. He shook his head. 'Thrown away like garbage,' he said softly.

'Yep.' Jilly looked up at Dan. 'You okay, partner?'

'Yeah, this one's just a little raw.' He looked around at the street, the buildings. 'Pretty crumby neighborhood. Not much left around here.'

'The buildings are just being left to rot, mostly. A store here and there: pawnshop, liquor store. There's a few families, a lot of homeless squatting in the buildings. I wouldn't be surprised if there are a few suspicious arsons regularly.' Jilly continued her intent scan of the woman's body.

Dan sighed deeply. 'Lots of drug traffic around here at night, they tell me.'

'She doesn't look like a local,' Jilly said.

'Not exactly a squatter.' The victim was a small woman, perhaps five foot three. She wore a pair of khakis and a pale green button-down shirt. The shirt was expensive and clean, except for a blood stain on the collar. She had one camel-colored slip-on canvas shoe; her left foot was bare. There were random blood stains on various parts of all her clothing, as well as what looked and smelled like remnants of trash from the bin she had been stuffed into. Her hair was ash-blonde and shoulder-length, now matted, tangled and tinted with blood. Her face was bruised and swollen, especially her cheeks and nose. There were rivulets of dried blood along her nose, cheek and jawline. Jilly reflected that even after many years, she could not become inured to this. She forced herself to tunnel-focus on the dead woman's clothing and began to systematically check the pockets.

'Mickey was right. Doesn't seem to be any kind of ID. Nothing in her pockets at all. No jewelry of any kind, no rings, no necklaces, bracelets ...' She ran her fingers through the woman's hair to reach the right earlobe, then did the same on the other side of her head. 'Her ears are pierced but no earrings. In fact the lobes are torn. Whoever did this may have ripped them right off of her ears. It looks as if it was done after she was already dead.'

'Robbery seems a strong possibility,' Dan said, watching Jilly and making notes. Jilly knew from experience that he was quietly making his own observations as he let her work, and his notes would be thorough.

'Certainly looks like it. She's nicely dressed. What was she doing here?' Jilly shot a look around them to emphasize her point.

Now she inspected the dead woman's hands. 'Manicures. There are what look like defensive wounds. But look — nice, clean, even nails. Maybe she got something from her assailant under those nails though.'

Dan bent down to peer at the fingers that Jilly gently held up and spread apart. 'Cuts, scratches, bruises ... but ... what are those dark blue stains on her fingers?'

'They look like ink, maybe from a felt-tip pen? Mickey will tell us more.' She continued to scrutinize various parts of the body, handling the lifeless woman as gently and respectfully as she could — almost tenderly. After this horrible treatment, Jilly somehow felt that she owed that much to her. Finally, she arranged the woman carefully, took out her smart phone, and snapped several photos of her face, trying to show as little of the damage as possible and to capture a clear likeness in case they found someone who could identify her. There was no way to completely obscure the beating she had taken.

When she was done, Jilly put away her phone and just looked at the body for a long moment. 'Whoever this guy was, this was personal. There's a major degree of anger in this attack. He was still beating her after she died.'

She wanted to make a silent promise to the woman lying on the ground, that she would find whomever had done this and speak for someone who could no longer speak for herself. But she knew from experience that it might be an empty promise, and that made her surprisingly angry this time.

Dan turned to the pile of detritus that had been removed from the can. An SID technician was still meticulously sifting through it, taking photos. 'Anything of hers in that stuff, I wonder?' He stood up and took a few steps towards the investigator.

The tech looked over his shoulder through goggles at Dan, lowered his camera, and nodded. 'Almost done here, Detective. Doesn't really look like much. Mostly garbage — food scraps, bottles and cans, stuff like that. And of course the inevitable, less savory stuff. Some drug stuff like a needle, a piece of a pipe. Other material I don't need to tell you about.'

'Uh, yeah. Thank you for that, we get the picture.'

'We did find her other shoe.' He pointed among the banana peels, greasy paper bags, and unidentifiable debris to a slip-on that was an obvious match to the one found on the victim. 'Nothing else that seems likely to have come from her.'

'No items of jewelry, nothing that might have come from a handbag or a wallet then, nothing that might help us ID her?'

The SID man shook his head.

'Was the body on the top of the bin?'

The tech shrugged. 'Apparently so. The

driver saw the body in there. He stopped the dump in mid-motion and brought it back down, and she fell out. The victim must have been doubled over and jammed into the container.'

'I assume you're checking the other bins along the street as well.'

'Of course.' He pointed down the street to two other jump-suited figures who had upended two other containers and were poring over their contents.

Jilly stood up and joined the conversation. 'Is that the driver over there near the truck? He's the one who found her?' The tech nodded.

Jilly carefully replaced the tarp over the body. They stripped off their gloves and walked down the street. A husky dark-skinned man in a blue coverall, his hair still full but greying, stood up from his seat at the curb. He had been talking with a female officer; they both turned as Jilly and Dan approached.

The officer smiled. 'Well, Detective Lee, fancy meeting you here!' She looked at Jilly, almost as a second thought, and nodded. 'And Detective Garvey.'

'Officer Kovetsky.'

Jilly swore she saw Dan's face redden a little. She remembered the youthful woman patrol officer from other scenes and cases, and clearly she and Dan remembered one another. Kovetsky was considerably more seasoned than she looked; she had worked some of the city's harshest neighborhoods for a few years now.

'This is Delino Washington,' Kovetsky said. 'He discovered the body this morning.'

Jilly turned to him. 'Mr. Washington, thank you for waiting. I know this must have been an imposition on your time.'

Washington shrugged stoically. 'I can't take the truck anyway until your crew is done with it. Or rather they can't send somebody to come get it from me until they get the okay from you guys. And to tell you the truth, I'm still on the clock.'

'So tell us what happened this morning.'

'I was running my usual Monday morning route through here. As I hoisted that can over there, I could tell it had something heavy in it. Nothing all that strange about that. You'd be amazed at the stuff people throw in those things.'

14

Jilly wondered how much worse it could have been.

'I've done this long enough that I can kind of judge just how much weight is in the container. I figured I'd better check on just what it was, and I sorta peered through the window. As the lifting arm went up, I saw what looked like a *leg* sticking out. It just freaked me out, and I hit the return lever. The can went flying back down to the street with a bang, tipped over as the arm released it, and — well, she came out.' He hesitantly jerked a thumb towards the body.

Dan picked up the questioning as he jotted in his notebook. 'Did she fall completely out of the container?'

'No ... it kinda looked as if she'd been wedged in there. The force of the impact jarred her loose but she only came out partway.' Washington ran a thick hand over his eyes for a moment. 'She was sort of bent in half, stuck in butt-end first. Oh ... excuse me, that's disrespectful to the lady. That just sorta came out.'

Jilly decided she liked the guy. He seemed a decent sort. 'That's okay, Mr. Washington, we understand. What did you do next?'

'I just sat there for a while, you know? It was a shock. Finally I got out of my truck and went over to make sure I'd actually seen what I thought I had. I saw her there, her body sticking out, her eyes staring right up at me. I didn't know what to do, don't know how long I just stood there. I looked around and there was nobody else on the street. Finally I figured out I should call somebody.' He pulled a cell phone out of his coverall pocket and held it up. 'I called the cops. I mean, you guys. Then I called work. They all told me to stay here until they showed up.'

'Not a neighborhood you want to stand around in,' Dan noted.

'That's for sure,' Kovetsky interjected.

Washington nodded. 'Word on that, Detective. But I didn't exactly have a lot of choice. I decided in any case I would probably rather be standing along this little side street, and it was early enough in the morning that there wasn't much chance of any trouble showing up. Those guys crawl back into their holes and go to sleep when the sun comes up.'

Dan was sweeping his gaze completely

16

around in a circle at the surroundings. 'This looks like a war zone here. Where's all the trash coming from in these receptacles?'

'There are businesses around here,' Washington said. 'Mostly bars and junk shops. Some people actually live here. And, to tell the truth, people bring their trash here from other parts to dump it.' He pointed down the street where two decaying mattresses sat atop a pile of unrecognizable plastic and wood items. 'I've even found piles of building material dropped here by construction companies. This neighborhood is the city's Dumpster.'

Not hard to detect the contempt in Washington's voice for the area, or the fact he was highly unsettled. Hard to blame him. Jilly noticed that Dan paused in his writing for a moment at the comment and looked around at the heap of dumped refuse.

Jilly continued, 'Did you touch or move the body or any of the contents of the container after that?'

Washington looked a little sheepish. 'Well, a little. Like I said, I wasn't really thinking straight. I kinda pulled her out a little bit, just to be sure it wasn't a mannequin or something like that, you know? Those things can be really lifelike. I may have scattered some of the trash out on the street. I don't remember.'

'Okay. We're going to have to get your prints so we know which ones are yours.'

'Am I going to have to take more time to go down to the station and do that?' Washington asked.

'Maybe not. One of the techs ought to be able to do it right here.'

He looked relieved. 'Well, then. Sure. Of course.'

'And you have no idea who this woman is, right?'

'Hell, no. How would I? Never seen her before.'

'You didn't find anything that might help to identify her?'

'Oh, no. No. No.' He raised his hands and his eyebrows. 'Didn't take nothing. I tell you, I've got nothing to do with this!'

Jilly raised her own hands in placation. 'I'm not saying you did, Mr. Washington. We're just hoping to find something to ascertain who she is. At the moment we've got no idea.'

'I wish I could help you, Detective. Nobody should die that way.' He shook his head sadly. 'Treated like another piece of garbage.'

'Look who's here,' muttered Dan. Jilly looked around to see the van arriving, just outside the yellow police tape, emblazoned with the colorful logo of one of the local television stations. One of the directing officers had motioned for it to stop and was walking over to talk to the driver.

'How did they get word of this so fast?' Jilly said. Surprisingly to Dan, she uttered an epithet he did not often hear coming from her. She had been hoping for at least a little lead time before the news hit.

Kovetsky turned in the direction of the van. 'I can go hold 'em off for a while for you.'

'No,' sighed Jilly. 'We'll go talk to them.'

Another aspect of a case like this that she hated, but knew she had to do.

2

Lieutenant Hank Castillo sat back in his chair, slightly rocking, his fingertips pressed together against his lips, as he watched the screen of the laptop that Jilly had laid on his desk. It was a video feed of the afternoon news from a local television station. A carefully coiffed and serious-looking woman stared into the camera over the top of a huge microphone bearing the numeral 8.

'The identity of the victim has not yet been publicly announced, pending notification of the family of the deceased. Detectives are withholding specific information for the moment but promise that more will be forthcoming shortly. Letitia Nevins, Channel 8 news, reporting from the Sheffield district.'

Jilly tapped a key and the video window closed on her screen. She folded up the laptop. She and Dan looked at Castillo and waited.

Castillo sat forward and rested his

forearms across his desk. As usual the coat of his three-piece suit was draped over the back of his chair, but even in shirtsleeves he bore the air of a dapper and authoritative sort. His greying temples gave him the air of both dignity and weariness. He stared alternately at both Dan and Jilly from under his thick eyebrows and scowled through his dense mustache.

'So what do you have?'

'No ID yet,' said Jilly. 'She had no identification of any kind, no jewelry. It appears that she was robbed. There are lots of pawnshops in the neighborhood. We canvassed as many as we could and had the unis do the same, to see if anybody had tried to sell jewelry. No luck so far. We're hoping that SID and the ME will come up with something we can use. For once we might luck out there and get some results reasonably quickly.'

'No witnesses, I'm assuming. Not in Sheffield.'

'Nobody we can find as yet. We've got unis trying to track down locals. Even on a Sunday night there must have been some traffic around there, buying and selling.

Nobody's going to own up to being there, of course.'

Castillo stared as if he expected more. There really wasn't much more. Dan finally spoke up, referring to his notes. 'The garbage bins are put out by the buildings along that street. There are three buildings on the that side of the block, all owned by the same company, whose offices are miles away on the other side of town. The buildings are largely empty. All told, there might be four or five habitable apartments in all of them along with a couple of small storefronts. Not enough to merit big metal garbage hoppers that would be picked up by private haulers that charge a monthly fee. They just put out the plastic bins and let the city pick up every week. We'll be checking with the building management but we don't expect it to be of any help. This seems pretty clearly to be a body dump.'

Castillo sighed deeply. 'Better make this your priority. We need to know who she is. This has the potential for nasty publicity. Upper-class woman, lurid and violent death in a seamy neighborhood. Your gal Letitia will be all over this by tomorrow, maybe even tonight. So will the other channels.' He shot them a piercing look. 'I don't need to tell you that pressure flows downhill here. I'll be getting it from above shortly. And that means you'll be getting it from me.'

Jilly nodded gravely. She looked at Dan as Castillo turned his attention back to the papers on his desk. That was his way, the squad personnel had learned, of indicating that the interview was over. They stood without another word. Jilly gathered up her laptop and followed Dan out the door.

The Personal Crimes Unit was unusually quiet this afternoon. Usually by midday the place was bustling with purposeful activity; there was seldom a letup from the onrush of new business being dropped in their laps from their frenetically challenging city. For some reason at this moment, there was a noticeable lack of the accustomed sound and fury. A number of the regulars seemed to be out of the squad room right now.

Years earlier, the unit had officially been called Special Crimes and before that had gone by the prosaic but accurate title Robbery-Homicide. At some point, the department had decided Personal Crimes bore more gravitas. The unit still dealt with basically the same types of crime, almost entirely felonies: homicides, severe assaults, robberies. Simultaneously, the unit that handled burglaries and similar non-violent crimes, currently housed in a similar squad room one flight up from them, had gained the moniker Property Crimes. The veterans of either unit would likely have remarked that there had been little difference in their function beyond the name changes.

For what it was worth, they could at least hear themselves think right now. All they needed was a viable strategy to think about.

They settled on Dan's desk and Jilly pulled up a nearby chair. They wracked their brains for the remainder of the afternoon.

★　★　★

It was early Tuesday morning. Dan had hardly settled in at his desk before his phone was ringing.

'Detective Lee.'

'Hey, Dan. Sandy Kovetsky here.'

'Officer Kovetsky. What's up?'

'I've told you before, you can call me

Sandy, okay? I think we may have hit some good luck on your Tustin Street murder.'

Dan grabbed a pen and pulled one of the ever-present legal pads in front of him at his desk. 'Tell me about it!'

'Guy got picked up for holding and dealing last night in a nearby neighborhood. Turns out he had some credit cards and IDs in his possession that weren't his. At any rate, he couldn't convince anyone he was a Jessica.'

'The name on the cards was Jessica?'

'Jessica Pidgeon.' She spelled the surname. 'He had an ATM card, an Amex card, a couple of store cards — even a driver's license. The guy's a noted reprobate around the area. So I made a point to go look at the cards. There are pictures on the license and a couple of the credit cards. Sure looks like it could be our girl.'

Dan scribbled the name down. 'Can you email over a scan of the photos on the cards?'

'Sure. Give me an addy.'

Dan recited his email address. 'You've still got him, right?'

'Oh yeah. We're holding him good and

tight here at Central Division.'

'Jessica Pidgeon. Did he have any other items, like jewelry, anything?'

'Nope. Just the cards. Not even any cash on him. He claimed he found a wallet on the street and took the cards and threw the rest away. He couldn't remember exactly where he threw them, just a general vicinity of a few blocks. We've got a couple officers looking right now.'

'When did he say he 'found' this wallet? Sunday night, Monday?'

'He's not the most compos mentis guy on the block, you know? He told the arresting officers it might have been Sunday night or maybe it was Saturday night, or maybe he's had 'em for a while.'

'If he really did throw a wallet in the trash Sunday night, it would have gotten picked up in the trash collection Monday. But it's worth a try, you're right. I appreciate that.'

'You can come on by at your convenience. Call Finley over here. You know him?'

'Sergeant Finley. I remember him. How's he doing these days?'

'Finley's Finley. You can ask him yourself. And I'll let you know if we have any luck on our canvass for the wallet. And I'm going over to check in myself. If you want to come join in dumpster diving, feel free.'

The thought didn't appeal to Dan and he trusted Kovetsky's judgment. 'Sounds like you've got it covered. Has anybody made any attempt to contact the woman who owns the cards or the license?'

'We're holding off pending your decision as to whether this is the victim.'

'So what *is* this guy's name who had the cards?'

'You're not gonna believe this. Marmaduke.'

'What?'

'I'm not kidding. That's his street name, Marmaduke.'

'Anybody know his real name?'

'He wasn't carrying any ID of his own. He told them his name is Marmaduke Jones. And it turns out, viola, he's actually got a record under that name!'

Dan continued to scribble. 'Happen to know what kind of record? Violent crimes?'

'Possession, possession with intent to sell, an assault rap. I don't know any of the details. I got a look at the guy. He's a big dumb one. Certainly capable of the kind of assault we're talking about.'

'And they picked him up dealing? Where?'

'Maybe five, six blocks from where the victim was found. Marmaduke's apparently a freelancer. There was a disagreement going on between him and a couple of the local establishment boys who were unhappy about his encroaching on their territory. The conversation got loud and emotional and involved baseball bats. A few of our guys happened to be in the neighborhood, who interrupted them and chased them down. Possibly saved Marmaduke's life, for what that's worth.'

'Thanks, Off — uh, Sandy. I appreciate the heads-up. We'll get right on this and be over this morning.'

'Sad to say, Dan, after I send this over to you, I'm on my way out the door so I'll miss you. If you want me, I'll be up to my neck with the dumpster crew.'

'Likely a fool's errand, I'm afraid.'

'Maybe so, but it must be done. Talk to you later.'

Dan stood up and turned to Jilly's

desk. He noted that she was also on the telephone, earnestly absorbed in her own conversation, jotting on a pad. As he approached, she hung up and looked up at Dan. She read his expression and raised her eyebrows in expectation.

'Just heard from Kovetsky. Central Division picked up a guy last night with a pocketful of stolen credit cards and ID. Could belong to our victim.'

'And that was Mickey. The autopsy is finished. He'll send me over the results. His original estimate of TOD stands. He's figuring she died around eleven Sunday night. Looks as if she was beaten pretty savagely, with a hard blunt instrument like a cane or a club.' Jilly ran a hand through her short red hair, stared into some indeterminate distance, and exhaled deeply. It might have been morning but she looked weary already. She finally looked up again at Dan. 'Do we have a name on the cards?'

'Yeah. Jessica Pidgeon. She's sending me over scans.' Dan filled her in on the information he had been given by Kovetsky.

'Okay, so we need to trace her down and see what we find, and we need to go over and talk to this perp.'

There was a 'ding' from Dan's computer. He walked back over to his desk, tapped some keys, and said, 'Sandy sent over the scans of the IDs.'

'Sandy, is it now,' said Jilly as she rose to join him.

'C'mon, don't start, Jilly. She asked me to call her that.' He brought up two of the images side by side on his monitor: the driver's license and the photo on the back of the Amex card.

'Uh-huh,' she muttered as she stood next to him and peered at the screen. She pulled out her phone and opened up the photos she had taken of the victim. They stared back and forth at the two screens silently for a long time.

'It's her,' Jilly said finally.

'Yeah. I agree.'

Jilly sighed again. 'I guess we start with the address on the license.'

'It's Farmington,' Dan read, referring to a nice upper-middle-class suburb to the north of the city. He sat down and started tapping on his keyboard once again, beginning the search for whatever information they could find on Jessica Pidgeon.

'Someone filed a missing persons on her yesterday. A James Pidgeon, same address.' Dan scanned the information. 'Her husband. Filed with the Farmington police department.'

'I guess that's where we start. Anything else coming up on her?'

'Nothing of consequence.'

'Let me get that contact phone number,' Jilly said, leaning in. Under the circumstances a telephone call was clearly out of the question; they needed to do this in person. But they had been able to find the husband. Jilly knew this drill way too well. She would call the husband, tell him simply they were calling in regard to his missing persons report, and ask to meet in person.

Luckily the number belonged to James Pidgeon's cell phone and he answered immediately. He was at work but would meet them at his house within the hour. Jilly expertly fielded his attempts to question her further but there was a certain level of apprehension in this kind of situation that could never be dispelled.

Their morning was clearly set out for

them: first James Pidgeon, then Marmaduke Jones at Central Division. There was always the hope that a case like this could be cleared up quickly and neatly, to bring some closure to the horrified family of the victim. In this instance, Jilly doubted it. The circumstances were too peculiar.

They checked in with Lieutenant Castillo and brought him up to speed on their recent findings and their plans. He gave them the green light and reiterated that this case took primacy over everything else.

'I know you'll handle the interview with the husband with tact and delicacy,' Castillo said pointedly, casting a tight smile at Jilly.

'Yes,' Jilly replied with equal wryness. 'You do know that, Lieutenant.'

Castillo raised his hands in mock surrender. 'I have every faith in you, Detectives. Now go and solve this pain-in-the-neck case for me. And keep me updated. There are inquiring minds that want to know.'

* * *

They took the elevator down to the parking garage. 'You want to drive?' Jilly asked.

'I'm good with you driving. While we're on our way over, I'll call Finley and arrange for us to meet the suspect afterward.'

'I've noticed you don't seem to want to do much driving lately,' Jilly observed.

'You've got a heavier foot than me,' Dan said, pulling out his phone and thumbing through his contact numbers. 'And we're in a hurry.'

The Pidgeon residence was one of several large Spanish Colonial-style houses, all with red tile roofs, along a winding, sycamore-lined street in the hills north of the city.

'Nice neighborhood,' Dan commented as they drove up the hill.

'Certainly is. Comfortable living.'

'And our job right now is to make it terribly uncomfortable. I hate this part. That's the house, on the right, 1220 Coventry.'

'And you're not going to stop hating it,' Jilly muttered as she pulled to the curb in front of the house. 'Trust me.'

A tall, florid and freckly man with thinning red hair threw open the door scant seconds after they had pressed the doorbell. 'You're the police?' he said breathlessly.

'Here about my wife?'

Jilly nodded. They both already had their ID and badges out to show him. He hardly looked.

'Please, come in, come in,' he urged, closing the door behind them. 'Do you have any information on her? Do you know where she is or what happened?'

'Mr. Pidgeon,' began Jilly gently, 'let's all go sit down. Are there children in the house at the moment, or anybody else?'

'No, no. They're visiting their grandmother in Pennsylvania. There's just me. What's happened? Is she all right?'

They walked into the living room and Pidgeon anxiously waved to chairs for them to sit in.

'First of all, we have to find out if it's actually your wife that we're here about.' Jilly took a seat close to Pidgeon and took out her phone.

'There's no easy way for us to do this. I have to caution you, the photo I'm going to show you could be upsetting. I'm sorry, but this is all we have to go on.' She tapped up one of the photos of the victim and slowly handed it to him. 'Is this your wife, Jessica?'

He began to nod but then he stopped. He saw the context of the picture. He stared at it blankly for a very long time, saying nothing, not reacting at all.

They waited.

'Oh my God,' he finally said hoarsely. 'Is she ...?'

'Mr. Pidgeon, is this your wife, Jessica?' Jilly asked.

He nodded vigorously, pursing his lips, unable to speak. They could see the tears begin to well in his eyes.

'I'm sorry, but ... you're absolutely positive?'

Continuing to nod silently, he handed back the phone to Jilly.

'I'm very sorry, Mr. Pidgeon.'

He suppressed several silent sobs, then found his voice. 'What happened?'

Jilly cautiously provided a few more details. She had done this too many times in the past. 'We're still trying to figure that out, sir. She was found on a side street in the city very early Monday morning. She was killed and left there Sunday night.'

'Where? Where in the city?'

'Tustin Street. It's in the area called Sheffield.'

'Sheffield! I've heard of Sheffield, but we don't go through there, not ever. What was Jessy doing there?'

'We don't know yet, sir. We're trying to find out the whole story. I know this is awfully hard, but are you up to answering some questions for us now? It could help us a lot.'

'No, that's fine. I mean, yes. I mean … yes, I'll try.'

'Thank you, Mr. Pidgeon. If this gets to be too much, let us know and we'll stop. When was the last time you saw Jessica?'

'Friday evening. I drove the kids to the airport.'

'You didn't see your wife all weekend?'

'No. I had a business trip. I got on a plane myself that night and came back very late Sunday.'

'Just curious, what kind of work do you do?' asked Dan. He was not writing; he was listening, applying a lesson he had learned from Jilly about observing body language and subtle cues.

'Computer tech. I'm in computer tech.'

'So you travel a lot, you're away from home often?'

'These days, yes. I helped establish a small startup. It's about to be bought, so I travel a lot.'

'So Jessica was alone here all of last weekend. Was that unusual?'

'I'm gone a lot these days. The kids are usually around ... well, they're out a lot. Brad is fourteen and Laurie is sixteen and they're both busy kids. There used to be a housekeeper, but she's no longer working here.'

'A housekeeper?' Dan asked.

'Yes, but she left our employ last week. She hasn't been here in a week or so.'

'Can you tell us about her? Had she worked for you long?'

'Melinda. Melinda Barstow. She worked for us for — oh, about ten or twelve years or so. She also provided child care when the kids were younger. She was here five days a week, sometimes more. She was like a member of the family.'

'But she left last week? Did she resign?'

'No. There was some disagreement with my wife. Jessy fired her.' Pidgeon shot a look at both of them. 'You aren't thinking … no, I couldn't believe Melinda could have done anything to harm Jessica. Never.'

Dan now opened his notebook and began to write. It was Jilly's cue to take over. 'Do you know where we might contact her?' she asked.

'Offhand, no. Jessy kept the information, and it would take me a while to … wait. Melinda called me the other day.' He took his own phone out of his pocket and tapped the screen a few times. 'Here's the number she called me from.'

Jilly opened her own phone and noted the number he was showing her on the screen. 'Why did she call you?'

He struggled, haltingly, to reply. 'She said that Jessy wouldn't talk to her and she wanted me to help smooth things out between them. She said she would need a letter of reference from us, that Jessy was refusing and could I help. She called me twice, in fact. I told her I'd talk with Jessy. I didn't know what happened. I never got to talk to her about that. I still don't know.' He heaved a sigh and his eyes seemed to focus on a far corner of the living room. 'I guess I never will. The kids aren't supposed to return until Friday. I'll have to call the grandmother and tell her. Oh my God, this is awful.'

'They're with your wife's parents?'

'Her mother, yes. In Pennsylvania.'

'What would Jessica do when she was by herself here? Did she ever go anywhere, socialize with friends anyplace particular?'

'She had friends here in the neighborhood. I guess maybe other wives, parents from the school. Sometimes she'd go out to lunch. We belong to a golf and tennis club. She'd go there to swim or play tennis or have lunch now and then.'

'You weren't with her at the club?'

'I'm too busy to go anymore. She always liked the club thing more than I did anyway. It was her and her friends.'

'Was she close to anyone in particular?'

'Dory Snyder, up the street. I remember her. Tamara Marsh, at the club. I don't know who else specifically.'

'Other parents, perhaps, from the kids' schools?'

'No. She hadn't had much to do with other parents in some time now.'

'Did she go into the city very often?'

'No, not really. She tended to stay in Farmington. I can't think of any reason she would have been down in the city that night. Certainly not in that area.'

'I assume she had a car, right?'

'Yes. A grey Audi sedan. Two years old. It's not here. It was gone when I returned from my trip.'

'Do you have the information on that, sir? Perhaps the registration, or the title?'

Pidgeon raised his hands, looking disoriented. 'I don't know. She might have kept the registration in the car.'

'Okay, we can get that from the DMV. The car was registered in her name at this address?'

'That's right.'

'Did she tend to carry a lot of money with her, anything valuable? Did she wear jewelry?' Jilly thought about the earrings that had been ripped from the woman's earlobes.

'Some. I had given her some earrings she liked. She wore a ring that her mother had given her that had sentimental value. Sometimes she wore a gold necklace with a pendant.'

'Is there any chance you could describe any of those?'

'They were all gold. She liked real gold. She tended to like hangy earrings, like teardrops or things like that ... maybe this big.' He indicated with thumb and forefinger. 'The ring had a couple of stones set into a plain gold band. I don't know, maybe sapphires? They were blue. The necklace was a plain chain, a circular pendant with a stone. That was blue too.' Pidgeon stopped and looked down. They could tell he was beginning to tremble. 'I can't understand how someone could do something this horrible to her. Maybe we need to stop now.'

'Of course, sir. One last thing, you can't think of anybody who would be capable of doing this to your wife? Anybody at all?'

Pidgeon shook his head and said nothing. When he looked up them, his eyes were red.

Jilly handed him one of her cards, and Dan followed suit. 'We'll be in touch, and you can call us at any time, if you think of anything that might help us find whoever did this, or if you just want to talk. And if it might help, we can suggest people who might be able to help you through this.'

'Grief counselors,' Pidgeon said quietly.

'One of the things I was thinking of, yes. Is there anybody we can contact for you, anything we can do?'

Pidgeon said very quietly, 'No. No, thank you.' He lowered his head and sat mute. Finally he said, 'I'm sorry, do you mind …'

'No problem, Mr. Pidgeon, we can show ourselves out. We're very sorry for your loss.'

★ ★ ★

'What's your take on Mr. Pidgeon?' Jilly asked as they drove back down the hill past well-trimmed lawns and trees.

'I'm really not sure,' Dan said pensively, staring out the window. 'I'm not getting a sense that he and his wife were all that close. What about you?'

'The story's kind of strange, I'll give you that. He's gone a lot, the kids are gone, nobody in the house all week. Even the housekeeper's gone.'

'He seemed to take it all pretty well, all things considered. That kind of news is a real gut shot. But shock does funny things to people.'

'Yes. Sometimes it takes a while to set in.'

'We've got to look at him. Something's not right. I just can't put my finger on what.'

'Agreed, partner.'

'And we'll need to get some more names of the people she hung around with. And talk with the women he mentioned.'

'And I really want to talk to that house-keeper,' Jilly continued. 'The one that Jessica had the argument with. So ... off to Central Division. At least we've got some kind of lead, this Marmaduke character.'

Dan sighed before answering. 'It'd be nice if it turned out that easy.'

'But? I sense a 'but' ...'

'I don't know, Jilly. This guy turns up with all of her credit cards and ID in his pocket. Even if he turns out to be good for this, it leaves so much unanswered.'

Jilly nodded. 'I see what you're saying.'

'If this is just a robbery that went bad ... the big question is, what was Jessica Pidgeon from Farmington doing down in Sheffield at night?'

'Let's take this one thing at a time, Dan.

We can only answer one question at a time.'

'I'll tell you what's on my mind though. Remember how Delino Washington was taking about the neighborhood being a dump site?'

'Sure. He clearly hates that area.'

'It makes a lot more sense if she was killed somewhere else and dumped there.'

'Could be. There was no car, nothing else connected with her on the scene, just what was on the body itself. Maybe the evidence will tell us more. When we go back the detailed autopsy results from the ME should have come through, and maybe SID will have something for us as well.'

'I wish we had some of that to go on now before we talked to Marmaduke.'

'Everything falling into place in just the right order? Yeah, that happens a lot … in the books and the TV shows. Let's see how this plays out. In any case he's not going anywhere.'

★   ★   ★

'So how have you been, Sergeant Finley?' Jilly asked as she signed in at the holding area. 'I believe you know my partner, Dan Lee.'

Finley, a hefty, ruddy-faced veteran, stretched his mouth into a sardonic smile. 'Living the dream, Detective, always fun and games down here. And yourself?' He nodded at Dan. 'You lucked out, Detective Lee. You got yourself a great partner.'

'Don't I know it,' Dan said.

'Aren't we all living the dream, though. So tell me about this guy.'

Finley smirked. 'A regular brain surgeon, this one. He's kind of a laughing stock in the local 'hoods. Always trying some new scheme that falls through.'

'His jacket looks like he's got a tendency to violence?'

'Yeah, he's done a few violent crimes. He's about as sweet as he is smart.'

'You think he's the kind of guy would do a mugging right on the street?'

'Never got him on that type of thing, but who knows?'

'What was he doing when he got picked up?'

'Peddling product on a boulevard, right in the middle of the Brown Street Skulls

territory. Figured he'd just be an entrepre-
neur and squeeze himself into their market.
Standing right out there kitty-corner from
one of the Skulls' own guys, flagging down
cars that were cruising through. Probably
took about three minutes for the Skull to
get on his burner and drop that old dime on
Marmaduke. A couple enforcer types pulled
up in one of their black SUVs and rolled
down a window and genius Marmaduke
asked them what they'd like. They were out
of the car with baseball bats like grass out
of a goose.'

'Batting practice on the freelancer. Very
educational. How'd he find himself delivered from their hands and in the gentle
loving ones of Central?'

'We happened to have an undercover
guy down there setting up a bust. This was
going to mess that up good, so he discreetly
got on the horn. He caught a nearby squad
car that broke up the home run derby.
Marmaduke took a few good shots before
they all saw the cruiser and turned tail to
run. The uniforms were able to run down
Marmaduke when he turned down a dead-
end alley.'

'And he was still holding. Didn't even have the sense to dump his stash then?'

'Well, he did try, but he didn't start to toss anything until he was actually in the blind alley.' Finley shook his head; his smile became more mirthful. He was enjoying the tale. 'Dumbest guy you ever met.'

'So they caught him holding, and they found the cards and the IDs of the victim on him as well?'

Finley reached into a drawer in the desk and pulled out a plastic bag, handing it to Jilly. 'Here you go.' He picked up a set of keys on the desk. 'So shall we go meet Prince Charming?'

*   *   *

He had been brought to an interview room that was even bleaker and more sterile than the ones in Personal Crimes. Marmaduke Jones was a large man, a baleful six-foot-four lump of dough with a shaved, notably lopsided head, a squinty left eye, and an aura of dumb malevolence. He sprawled back over his chair, handcuffed to the metal table in front of him, glowering at them through his red-rimmed good eye as they entered the interview room. Neither of the detectives sat down; they stood across the table, looking down at him.

'So, Marmaduke,' Jilly began. 'Is that really your name?'

'Call me Duke on the street,' he mumbled, his stare growing apprehensive as he shifted his gaze back and forth at the duo. Curiosity had begun to dawn as to why these two new cops had come to talk to him.

'That's not what we hear. We hear you're Marmaduke. And honestly, we're not hearing a lot of respect when you're called that.' She held up the plastic bag with the cards, by a corner between thumb and forefinger so he could see it. 'So what we want to know, Marmaduke, is how you came into the possession of these?'

He shook his head and tried to think for a long moment. 'Found a wallet. They were in it.'

Dan spoke up now. 'And you of course hung on to them so you could go find the rightful owner and return them.'

Marmaduke wasn't sure which one of the two to look at, so he kept looking back and forth. He shrugged. 'Maybe. Somethin' like that.' Even he could tell that sounded particularly lame, so he shrugged again. 'I hadn't decided, maybe I was gonna try to use them, get a few bucks out of them. Sometimes they don't cancel 'em right away.'

'So this wallet you say you found. Just where was that?'

The big man thought for a long time. 'I don't remember. Lyin' on top of a trashcan somewhere.'

'Just lying there, on top of a trashcan.'

'Yeah. Pretty sure.'

'What kind of trashcan, exactly?'

'You know, one of those big plastic ones out on the street?'

'And when was this you found the wallet exactly?'

He shook his head, looking confused. 'Don't remember. The other night.'

'It was at night? Or during the day?'

'I think it was night. The other night.'

'Last night? Night before last?'

'Sometime on the weekend, I think. Not really sure.' He ran his free hand over his face. 'I been a little confused the past few days, you know?'

'Using your own product, you mean,' Dan said. 'Getting high.'

Marmaduke just stared at the bag.

'So you found this wallet, full of these cards, just sitting on a garbage bin? What did the wallet look like?'

He waved his free hand around as if trying to catch a word out of the air. 'Like ... like a book, you know? It was kinda long and it opened up like a book. Had a snap-strap holding it together. Light brown, I think. Yeah, like a yellow-brown?'

Jilly broke in. 'What was it made of?'

More head-shaking and hand-waving. 'Maybe leather?'

'And what color was the garbage bin?'

He squinted at her. Whether he was trying to actually remember or to make up a believable story, it was obviously not coming very easily. 'It was dark. I don't know. Black probably. Most of 'em are black, aren't they?'

'So you found this wallet, and you decided to go through it and take out anything of value? Did you leave anything in it?'

'Don't remember. I think so. I think there were like pictures.'

50

'Was there money? You took money, didn't you?'

'Don't remember.'

'So if we find this wallet, it's going to have pictures and other things still in it, right? But no money. No credit cards.'

Dan returned to the questioning. 'What did you do with this wallet after you took everything out of it?'

'I tossed it. I don't remember where. Maybe back into the bin where I found it.'

Dan bent in closer to Marmaduke. 'The woman who owned those cards is dead. But you knew that, didn't you?'

'What?'

'You killed her. You didn't find her wallet on a garbage bin. You robbed her and killed her.'

'What? *No!*' The sulking heap of a man suddenly found some energy. His eyes opened wide, his voice raised. 'I didn't kill nobody! I've never killed nobody!'

'How do you know?' asked Jilly, folding her arms and glaring down at him. 'You say you don't remember much. You were high.'

'You took her jewelry too,' said Dan. 'And you beat her. A big guy like you, beating that little woman until she died. And then you just kept beating her.'

'I swear! I didn't rob that lady. I didn't rob any lady! I wouldn't hurt a woman, I wouldn't! I didn't kill anybody! I found that wallet, just like I told you!'

'Then you'd better start remembering better right away.'

Jilly softened her tone, rested her hands on the table, and bent closer to the big trembling man. 'If you want us to believe you had nothing to do with her death, then you need to give us something to prove your story. You see how this looks? You've got the victim's personal property and you can't account for how you got it? Come on. Tell us where to find something that backs up your story.'

'Don't remember. I just don't remember. I didn't kill nobody!'

'If you don't remember,' said Jilly, staring him straight in the eye, 'just how can you be so sure you didn't kill anybody?'

Marmaduke looked up and met her stare. This time he growled. 'I've never killed nobody in my life.'

'We saw your jacket. You've got quite a

history of violence.'

'Somebody messes with me, I stand my ground. Never hurt nobody who didn't have it coming. Never killed no one. And I don't hurt women.'

★　★　★

The ride back to their own station house was somber. They both sat in their own thoughts for much of the drive. Finally Dan broke the silence.

'He seems pretty good for this.'

Jilly sighed heavily. 'Maybe.'

'I'm hearing a 'but'.'

'I keep coming back to why she would have been down in that neighborhood to begin with.'

'The guy's got her cards and ID, he's got a history of violence. Fill it in a little bit more and … there are convictions on less than that.'

'I don't think so, Dan. It's not enough for a prosecutor. And it's not enough for me. Maybe he did it, but we need to fill in more of the details.'

'Back to the body dump, which seems

logical. So he robbed her somewhere else and brought her body there. The husband says her car isn't at the house. Maybe she was driving somewhere, parking, getting out of her car and he attacked her. Two-year-old Audi sedan. Nice car. Figured her for a rich one?'

Jilly sighed deeply. 'We need to find that car.'

They descended into a thoughtful silence. Finally Dan pulled out his smart phone, tapped at it for a minute, and then made a clucking noise.

'What?'

'Your pal Letitia must have decided to move on the story. Looks like there's something on the news this afternoon.'

'Don't tell me she's got a name.'

'Nope, but she tried sandbagging Captain Crowley this morning in front of headquarters when he arrived. The TV station's website has a video here of the conversation.' Dan turned up the sound. It was a short clip, but Crowley did a good job of stonewalling the newswoman, continuing his forward motion while feeding her some general statements that actually sounded pretty good: detectives having important leads but not wishing to release specifics pending family notification, that type of thing. Before she could follow up, he was out of microphone range, never hurrying or giving the appearance of concern, but suddenly being swallowed up by a mass of department associates, moving through the door into the station.

'Impressive,' Jilly remarked. 'The captain's a smoothie.'

'And Letitia's a tough one.'

'Tell me about it. I'm sure her competition's breathing down her neck on this. We need to get some public statements out there. At this point it's to our advantage to get Jessica's name out there. We need someone to come forward.'

Dan nodded. 'At least we've got plenty to potentially work on. With any luck, we'll have the full ME's report ... and if we're really lucky, maybe SID will have something for us as well. I'll run her records at Motor Vehicles and get the plate number so we can start putting out inquiries on the whereabouts of the car. Then I'll run Jessica's credit cards and see if anybody's used any of them.'

'I'll contact the housekeeper,' Jilly said. 'And then we should put the word out on the jewelry that the husband described, see if it's turned up in a pawnshop or anywhere else. And maybe your gal-pal Sandy knows some locals who can tell her something more about Marmaduke.'

Dan's wince was visible to Jilly even through the corner of her eye as she drove. 'My 'gal-pal'? Officer Kovetsky? Come on, Jilly, give me a break.'

'I don't know that I've ever seen a Chinese gentleman blush before. It's very sweet, actually.'

'She's just being friendly.'

'Uh-huh.'

'But even if that weren't the case … you've never had a patrol officer flirt with you?'

Jilly smiled brightly. 'I think I scare 'em away.'

'You scare *me* now and then. But seriously, none of that stuff with Officer Kovetsky or anybody else means anything.'

'Just my luck,' smiled Jilly, 'to get a partner who's fatally attractive.'

3

It was past lunchtime when they returned to the unit, but neither of them felt hungry as yet. Jilly figured it was the smell of the hunt; sometimes the urgency of a case just got to them this way. They both hit their desks and set to their tasks on telephone and computer. Dan entered the victim's name on the Department of Motor Vehicles website and immediately brought up the plate number for a two-year-old Audi A4 sedan registered to Jessica Pidgeon at 1220 Coventry Drive in Farmington. He jotted down the number on a legal pad, and immediately posted online alerts on the vehicle. Then he turned his attention to the transparent bag on his desk that held Jessica's cards. He pushed them around in the package so he could read the faces of the cards and picked up his telephone.

Jilly was a blur of multi-tasking. While jotting notes, she turned on her computer and picked up her desk phone. She tried the telephone number she had been given for Melinda Barstow and got an automated voice mail message. She left word to call her back, not leaving any other information. She ran phone number searches for Jessica's friends, Dory Snyder and Tamara Marsh. She found a Morris and Dory Snyder on Coventry Drive in Farmington, which clearly was the right family. She had no luck with a Tamara Marsh or a T. Marsh, and there were a dozen other Marshes in the general vicinity. Hopefully Dory Snyder would provide her further leads. She called the number and left another voice mail, asking Dory to return her call.

By now she had already brought up her email and discovered that Mickey Kendrick had indeed sent over the results of the autopsy of Jessica Pidgeon. Much of it confirmed the tentative information they had already garnered: time of death was around 11:00 p.m. on Sunday night. Cause of death was blunt force trauma to the head. The skull had been cracked. The victim bore marks and bruises on her body and head consistent with a beating by fists and a rounded hard object, perhaps the end of a stick or a bat, approximately two to three inches in diameter. Three of her ribs and bones in her arms and legs had been broken. Many of the blows had been delivered after death. Further damage had been done to the body post-mortem, probably by contorting it to fit it into the refuse bin. There were numerous finger marks on the arms where she had been held tightly. There was no chance of any kind of fingerprint but there was a good indication of the size of the hands of the assailant. The examiner's opinion was that one attacker was responsible.

Jessica's hands and forearms bore defensive bruises, as if she had tried to ward off blows, but there was no skin or other matter under her nails. That was too bad. Jilly had been hoping that somehow she had gotten some of her attacker's DNA.

She scrolled to the photographs. They were horrific. Jilly had seen things as bad and much worse, but something about these pictures, the sheer overkill being portrayed, curdled her stomach. 'You SOB,' she whispered. 'We will get you.'

Had Marmaduke Jones done this? He

was big enough, strong enough. He was the likeliest of suspects. But they would have to build their case to be sure and to ensure his conviction.

If the motive was robbery pure and simple, why batter her so savagely? Because he was high at the time, deranged?

A recurring theory came back to her again. 'This was personal,' she whispered to the picture on the monitor screen. 'Wasn't it? He knew you.'

'Got a hit on her ATM card,' Dan said, interrupting her macabre reverie. 'It was used to withdraw four hundred dollars around nine on Sunday night from a bank machine just over the city line from Farmington.'

'Four hundred?'

'That's the limit that can be taken out in one day. I spoke to the bank manager and she says there's a camera. We can go over and check it out.'

'Anything else of interest on the cards?'

'Not so far. I ran her recent credit history online and there doesn't seem to be any activity since Saturday. I've got a couple more calls to make but it's looking as if nobody's used any of her cards.'

'Okay, let me put out some alerts on the jewelry while you make those calls, then let's take a run up to that bank.'

'And I wouldn't mind maybe making a quick stop for a bite as well. I'm actually not that hungry but I think we're gonna be running all day. The trail's warming up.'

'A lot to be done. Want to split up?'

Dan hesitated. 'Naw, I think we're better off staying together for the moment, okay? Give me a holler when you're ready.' He turned and headed back to his desk.

Something, Jilly mused, was up with Dan. He usually was the first to suggest they head off in separate directions to cover more territory on a case like this. As soon as they had a spare moment she'd have to explore that with him. She turned back to her keyboard.

As they were leaving, Castillo came out of his office on a clear path to intercept them. Jilly rolled her eyes, hoping it was not noticeable from a distance. The Lou coming to you was never a good thing.

'You two make yourselves available in about two hours. Captain says we're

61

running an impromptu news conference on Jessica Pidgeon.'

Jilly nodded. 'Good idea.'

The corners of Castillo's mouth curled up under his mustache in a slight impersonation of a smile. 'And you two will be the stars. Run it by me what you plan to say before it starts.' He turned back to his office.

'Oh great,' muttered Jilly.

* * *

The 'quick bite' turned into takeout sandwiches that they consumed in the car on the drive to the Scully Boulevard branch office of Continental Interbank, at the north end of the city. The branch manager was ready for them and escorted them to the security office, where they were able to review a printout of Jessica's transaction from Sunday night and the video taken at the ATM that evening. They asked against hope if the bank kept any record of the serial numbers of bills dispensed from the machine, but as expected, the answer was no.

Jessica's account had been accessed at 9:52 p.m. They asked the manager to start the video at 9:50. It was a black and white video of medium-grainy resolution. There was a fairly static view of Scully Boulevard in harsh evening light with some traffic moving sporadically in the background. One or two pedestrians passed the camera without stopping.

'There,' said Dan.

A woman came into view from the left side, in a pair of light slacks and a pale tailored shirt. She was looking down at something she held in her left hand. A wallet, a large billfold style, open like a book. She reached into the wallet with her right hand and removed a card. The camera was above the ATM and slightly to the side, so as she approached the machine, it appeared she was looking off to their right and down. There was a serious, focused expression on her face as she extended her hand with the card, which disappeared out of camera as it slid into the machine.

'That's Jessica,' said Jilly.

They scanned the monitor to see if there was a sign of any other person, but nobody else was within view.

'Look,' said Dan. 'She's looking up at the camera. She knows it's there.'

Indeed, for a brief moment, Jessica's eyes starred directly at them, but she did not move her head, only her eyes. Then she looked back down, apparently entering her information into the keys on the ATM. When she was finished, her eyes once again glanced up at the camera without moving the rest of her head. She held the gaze for a beat, then looked back down again.

'She's taking the money,' Jilly said. 'And her ATM card.'

Jessica juggled the packet of bills and her card, taking a few seconds to successfully return the card to her wallet but still holding the bills. She stepped away from the machine, turning to their left and walking off camera quickly.

'She didn't take the receipt,' Dan noted.

'She looked right at the camera. Twice.'

'Maybe I'm reading too much into it. Maybe she was alone, and just being careful. But she seemed edgy and self-conscious. She only moved her eyes, not her head. Her movements were very controlled.

You'd think in a strange urban area at night, she'd be looking all around her. Maybe there was somebody else there who coerced her to take out the money?'

'Certainly possible. If so, they knew to stay to the side, well off camera. And maybe they warned her not to look at them or to give anything away.'

'If so, that's a smart gal,' said Dan. 'She played it cool but shot a couple of looks at the camera. Subtle, but maybe meaningful?'

'That could mean,' Jilly said grimly, 'that she might have figured she wouldn't have the chance to talk about any of this later. Maybe she had an idea of what was going to happen to her.'

★   ★   ★

The media conference was held in the station's small auditorium, which for occasions such as this was officially dubbed the 'press room.' In a brief consultation beforehand in Castillo's office, Captain Crowley had simply told them to lay out the bare facts and to field whatever questions followed by referring to the ongoing investigation.

It was brief and, to Jilly and Dan's relief, relatively painless. There were representatives of local television news stations and the city's last remaining newspaper. Jilly took the lead and kept to the facts, stressing the victim's name and an appeal for any information that might be of help. She stressed that there were further facts that needed to be kept confidential for the moment, and provided a number for possible tips or information. The follow-up questions were exactly what she expected: attempts to pry out another factoid or drop of information. She held her ground tactfully but firmly. Finally Crowley called an end to the conference and escorted the detectives and a handful of brass out of the room.

Once out of the auditorium, in a lobby that led to a side exit, Crowley said 'Nice job' to Jilly, nodded to them both, and walked off with his aides.

'Very nice,' said Castillo with a tight smile. 'You might be doing my job one of these days, Garvey.' And then he was gone as well.

Just like that, Dan and Jilly were alone

in the empty vestibule. The sudden silence descended on them like a late night snowfall. They stared at each other, momentarily stunned by the suddenness of it all.

'I agree,' smiled Dan. 'Good job, partner. Maybe you're destined to join the brass.'

'Oh, shut up,' sighed Jilly. 'Come on, let's get back to the real work.'

Jilly found a message at her desk that Dory Snyder had returned her call. Some things still worked the old-fashioned way around the unit. She picked up her desk phone and dialed the number that had been left for her. Jilly glanced at her watch. How had the day flown by that quickly? In a quick conversation, they made arrangements to meet at Snyder's home the next day.

*   *   *

Jilly had barely gotten to her desk Wednesday morning, and was trying to balance a mug of coffee while moving some papers on her desk, when her phone began to ring. She absently picked it up with her free right hand and held it to her ear.

'Detective Garvey.'

'Hello,' said a softly melodic voice on the other end of the line. 'You left a message for me to contact you. This is Melinda Barstow.'

Jilly grounded her coffee cup and switched the receiver to her left ear. 'Yes, Ms. Barstow, thank you for returning my call.'

'I heard about the murder of Mrs. Pidgeon. How horrible. I assume that's what this is in regard to.'

'Yes, it is. We'd very much like to talk to you and see if you can help us.'

'Of course. In fact, I received a letter in the mail from her this morning. I think you need to see it.'

'A letter, you say?'

'Yes. It's rather strange, and … well, it's easier if I show you.'

'Would it be convenient for us to come by and talk to you?'

'Certainly. I'm home all day.'

'We can come by right now if that's all right.' Jilly took the address from Melinda and hung up. She took a swig of her coffee, stood up, and walked to Dan's desk. He was absorbed in something he had pulled up on his monitor.

'Hey, partner,' she said. 'That was the housekeeper. She got something in the mail from Jessica.'

'The housekeeper?' Dan asked, momentarily confused. 'The mail? The *mail*? As in, post office, snail mail?'

'Does seem strange. In fact she used that very word. Come on, she's waiting.' She dropped the car keys onto Dan's desk. 'You get to drive this time.'

He hesitated. 'That's okay. I'm perfectly happy with having you drive.' He picked up the keys and handed them back to her as he rose from his chair. 'Let's go.'

Dan was several steps ahead of her heading to the stairs before she could say a word. Jilly started to call out to him but then stopped and shook her head. Whatever was up with him, it would keep.

Melinda Barstow's apartment building was on a well-kept street in a working-class neighborhood. There was a short set of stairs leading to a stoop. A handsome dark-skinned man in his thirties sat on the steps, reading a paperback book. He looked up as

Jilly and Dan approached from the street.

'Yes, can I help you?' he asked in a soft voice. He was an athletic-looking sort in a sweater and slacks. A pair of heavy horn-rimmed glasses gave an academic touch to his look.

'Is this where Melinda Barstow lives?' Jilly asked.

He eyed them back and forth with suspicion. 'And who might you be?'

Jilly had her badge out instantly, staring at him levelly. 'We're here to see Melinda.'

The man studied the badge for a moment before nodding and pointing back over his shoulder. He returned to his book as they walked past him to the doorway at the top of the stairs.

The door to the Barstow apartment was answered by a young woman, possibly a mature-looking teenager, in a sweater and jeans. Jilly and Dan showed their badges and identified themselves. Clearly they had been expected. The girl nodded and stepped back to let them into a small but scrupulously kept living room. She said, 'I'll get Mom,' and left the room. Dan and Jilly remained standing. They did not have long to wait.

'Detectives, how are you?'

Melinda Barstow carried herself with a palpable sense of dignity: posture erect, head straight, serious expression. She was lean, with dark hair and flawless beige skin, and dressed in a blazer and skirt in earth tones. She met them with a small relaxed smile and clear, intelligent hazel eyes that held their gaze with quiet confidence, then extended a hand and introduced herself formally. She invited them to two armchairs and deposited herself in a third, facing them across a low polished wood coffee table.

'I hope Olivia — my daughter — doesn't need to be here for this,' she said. 'She has the morning off from school. I asked her to stay in her room while we talk.' Now they noticed a definite trace of a Caribbean lilt to her voice.

Jilly nodded. 'That's fine.'

'That's quite a doorman you've got guarding the entrance,' Dan remarked.

Melinda looked momentarily confused, then smiled and laughed lightly. 'Oh, that must be Terry. He was out on the stairs, was he? A very nice man, very bright, well-informed. He's been a friend of ours for many years. That's something I like about this neighborhood. We watch out for one another. We're mostly immigrants around here, like myself. It's not a bad neighborhood, but there are some things you have to be careful of, you know? Especially a single mother with a daughter. We've got people like Terry who keep an eye out for all of us. He's quite protective. So did he require you to show proper identification in order to pass?'

Jilly smiled. 'He did regard us with some suspicion since we were strangers, yes.'

'It's our own version of a neighborhood watch. I appreciate the good people who keep us safe.' Melinda's bright expression darkened. 'I was terribly shocked to hear the news about Mrs. Pidgeon. I worked for her for many years, right up until recently. I left her employ under rather bad circumstances.'

'What do you mean, Ms. Barstow?' asked Jilly.

Melinda's brows knitted. She laced her fingers and rested her hands on the table. 'We had an argument that came out of nowhere. I still don't understand what happened. But she got terribly mad at me and fired me on the spot. She told me to leave her house immediately and not to come back. That was the last I ever saw her.'

'Just when exactly was this?'

A little over a week ago. Tuesday of last week.'

'You say you don't understand why she'd gotten so angry with you?'

Melinda shook her head. 'It was something she thought I'd done. Nothing big, as far as I could tell. She was picky lately about minor things. One time she took exception to the fact I'd made the kids hamburgers. She insisted on a lot of rules for their food: very little fat or sugar, no white bread, things like that. Lately she'd gotten kind of touchy about little things, and this was just another one of those. But she seemed to be already emotional over something that had happened, and she was irrational. She just blew up. It was so unlike her. She blew the issue totally out of proportion. I tried to reason with her, to calm her down, to explain my side of things, but she just exploded at me. She pulled some money out of her wallet and thrust it at me, said that would bring us up to date on my salary, and told me to pick up my things and leave and not to come back. The more I tried to get her to talk, the madder she got. Finally I just agreed and got my things and left. I figured in a day or two she'd come to her senses and call me back and we'd work out whatever the problem was.' She shook her head in a brief reverie. 'I worked for her and her family for twelve years and I treated them as I would my own family. I took care of the children as they grew. I was always honest and loyal. I thought she appreciated qualities like that.'

'And she never called you back or contacted you?'

'No. I tried to call her after a couple days, left her voice mails, but she never answered and she wouldn't return my calls. Once, I talked to Mr. Pidgeon. I thought maybe he'd have some idea what was wrong. The whole thing came as a total surprise to him.' She looked at the detectives with wide, uncomprehending eyes. 'It made no sense. It was hurtful to me. And then on top of that, I was really hoping I could get at least a reference from her if I had to go look for a new job. That's over twelve years I'd have to account for. It's not easy right now, the job market. A good employer reference would mean a lot. I don't think I could get work without one.'

'She refused to give you a reference?'

'She wouldn't even talk about it! Olivia is starting college in the fall. I need steady employment.'

Dan nodded. 'We understand, Ms. Barstow.'

'I saw on the news yesterday that Mrs. Pidgeon had been found murdered. That was terrible, just terrible. Poor woman. That place she was found, it made no sense. It's a dreadful place. And so far from her home. She didn't tend to leave Farmington, maybe now and then to drive to go shopping, but she was generally a homebody. And now this … this confounded me this morning was when this came for me in the mail.'

There was a manila envelope on the coffee table, which she now picked up. It was covered with stamps and an adhesive label on which an address had been desk-top-printed. She opened it and pulled out several sheets of text-filled paper.

'There was this letter,' she said, handing it to Jilly, who took it gingerly by a corner with her fingertips. She and Dan bent closer together to read it. It had likely been typed on a computer and then desktop-printed.

Dear Melinda,

Please forgive me for the terrible way I treated you. You did not deserve it after all the years of trustworthy service you showed me. All I can say in my own defense is that I have had many serious personal problems of late, and I have just not been myself. I have decided to enroll myself in a recovery program to address these. Please find enclosed here, a personal recommendation for your future employment and what I hope is a reasonable amount of severance pay to show my appreciation and help you through until you find new employment, as I know you will.

Fondly and sincerely,
Jessica Carpenter Pidgeon

Only the signature at the end was handwritten, in a dark blue ink that had spread into the fibers of the paper.

Melinda then held up three more sheets. It was a lengthy formal letter introducing Melinda Barstow and extolling her many virtues as an honest, upright, loyal, and capable woman who had managed the Pidgeon household in multiple ways. Again, everything had been typed on a computer, and was signed at the end by Jessica Carpenter Pidgeon with the same pen as the cover letter.

'And she sent you money as well? A check?'

'No, there was four hundred dollars in cash in the envelope.'

'Cash?'

'Yes. In twenties, bound together with a rubber band.'

'Was she in the habit of paying you in cash?'

'Yes, she always did. But she never sent it to me. She always handed it to me at the end of the week.' Melinda looked back and forth at them suddenly. 'I pay my taxes. I declare everything I make. I can't vouch for Mrs. Pidgeon, if she reported everything, but I'm on the level. And I'm a legal citizen.'

Jilly smiled and raised a hand in a gesture of reconciliation. 'Nobody's accusing you of any of that, ma'am. Just trying to get the facts here.'

'She mentions a recovery program,' Dan said. 'Was she in some kind of rehab? Did she have any kind of problem that you were aware of?'

Melinda shook her head. 'You mean like drinking or drugs or anything like that? No, certainly not that I was aware of. I was around the house a lot. She took a glass of wine now and then or maybe a small cocktail on a special occasion, but no.' She stopped and visibly bit her lip tensely, looking down at the table. A long uncomfortable silence fell upon the room.

'Ms. Barstow?' Jilly finally said gently. 'I think there's something on your mind. Maybe it will help to tell us about it.'

'She had problems with her marriage,' Melinda said quietly. 'She and Mr. Pidgeon were hardly speaking. He'd actually moved out a few weeks before that.'

'Moved out?' Jilly and Dan exchanged glances.

'He hadn't been living in the house for a while. He had an apartment somewhere in town, I think.'

'So there'd been some tension between them for some time, then?' Jilly asked.

'Oh yes. For months before he moved out, the house was unbearable. I never asked Ms. Pidgeon about it. I figured it wasn't my business. I tried to be supportive in, you know, more subtle ways.'

'So Mr. Pidgeon moved out, what, a month or two ago?'

'Let me think. Yes. Six weeks ago, this coming weekend. I remember he loaded up his SUV for a couple of trips. I generally don't work weekends, but I was asked to come on Saturday to help clean up after him.'

'Any idea what that might have been about?'

'Not my business, as I said.'

Jilly leaned forward with what she hoped was a conspiratorial look. 'Sure. But we all pick up on stuff going on at our place of business, don't we? I mean, I sure do. Stuff I'm not supposed to know. If you're smart, you can't help it.'

Despite herself, Melinda smiled. 'Where the bodies are buried, as they say.' She started suddenly and laid a hand across her mouth. 'Oh. Forgive me. That sounded … I mean, considering …'

Jilly laid her own hand over Melinda's other hand, the one that had remained on the table. 'No no, of course. Just an expression. But you understood what I was getting at. My point is that I bet you knew things about that household. You were considerate and discreet, and you acted professionally and responsibly. But you're also clearly a perceptive and intelligent woman, Ms. Barstow. I think you knew a lot about what was going on there.'

'I don't want to get anybody in trouble,' Melinda said hesitantly. 'It's water under the bridge now, all things considered.'

Jilly and Dan said nothing. They waited.

'Mr. Pidgeon, well … I think there may have been another woman. A younger lady. Maybe someone he worked with. I got the impression he was going to divorce Mrs. Pidgeon. They never talked about it in front of me, but there were little remarks, little references. An indirect barb here and there.'

'You thought they were in the process of divorcing?'

'I think so, yes, could be. Mrs. Pidgeon — well, she was increasingly on edge the past few weeks. Looked like she didn't sleep well some nights. She might have been drinking a *little* more, an extra glass of wine in her hand now and then, but it's not like I ever saw her tipsy or slurring her words or anything.'

'Did she act angry very often?'

'No. More like really quiet and somber. Distracted. Sometimes if I asked her a question, I'd have to repeat myself because she wasn't listening.'

'Can I go back to this letter for a minute?' Dan interjected. 'You say it wasn't usual for her to mail you things like this?'

'Never. This was the first letter I ever received from her in the actual mail. I'm surprised she knew my address. My phone number, certainly she knew. I mean, she has all my information, she might well have kept work records going back to my application. But I moved earlier this year. Of course I gave her the new address, but I got the impression she hadn't paid much attention at the time.'

'Is there anything odd about the fact she'd type such a personal letter to you instead of writing it by hand?'

Melinda thought about that, looking down at the letter. 'Well, she does have a computer. Once in a while she'd print out something. But if she needed to leave me a note or anything, it was always hand-written. As I said, she never sent me a formal letter like this before, so I'm not sure.'

'Does that definitely look like her signature?'

Melinda pulled the letter back, turned it around so it read right from her viewpoint, and peered at it carefully. She nodded at Dan. 'Yes. I'd say so.'

'She signed it with her whole name. Jessica Carpenter Pidgeon. I assume Carpenter was her maiden name?'

'Yes.'

'Was it her habit to sign her entire name like that?'

Melinda pondered that one thoughtfully. 'I honestly don't remember ever seeing her sign anything with her whole name like that. But I could be wrong.'

Jilly jumped back in. 'The last time you saw her — a week ago last Tuesday? — you said she was noticeably distraught? More than usual?'

'She was dramatically different that morning. Dramatically.'

Jilly nodded. 'You'd been at her house the day before, Monday?'

'Yes. I came Monday through Friday as a rule, usually got there around eight and left around six or seven, depending upon what needed to be done.'

'What would you generally do, was there a routine every day?'

'Pretty much so, yes. There was shopping for food and other necessities, laundry, general cleaning around the house, changing the linens, preparing meals. When their kids were younger, I'd do child care, drop them off at school, pick them up in the afternoon. Laurie, the older one, is midway through high school, and Brad is fourteen. They don't require anywhere near as much attention as when they were younger. Brad plays baseball on his school team, and now and then I'd still drive him to and from practice.'

'So you arrived at the Pidgeon home on Tuesday morning, and something was different with Jessica?'

'Well, she was very touchy all morning, but in a sulky way, do you know? Only speaking to me in a few syllables. Not that that was entirely unusual. She went out to run some errands or meet a friend or something. The real problem started when she returned later that afternoon.'

'How do you mean?'

'Laurie had a friend over to study. She was trying to help him. He's a very nice boy, trying to get through school and succeed, but it's as if everything is stacked against him.'

'So she was tutoring him?'

'Yes, kind of. Mrs. Pidgeon came home and exploded when she realized Laurie had a friend over. She started saying she knew I was 'conspiring' with Laurie, without her — Mrs. Pidgeon's — knowledge. She was firing odd questions at me about secret goings-on or something. None of it made any sense.'

'When you say 'conspiring' with Laurie — what do you mean exactly? What was she getting at?' Jilly asked.

'I'm still not really sure. It sounds as if she had discovered Laurie was doing something she shouldn't have. I tried to ask her what she meant: did she think I was smuggling in drugs to her, for Lord's sake? Or birth control? She kept saying that I knew what she was talking about.'

'I can see how that could be very upsetting to you.'

'Laurie and her friend came down into the kitchen. Mrs. Pidgeon chased the boy out of the house and had a screaming match with Laurie, who first tried to reason with her but lost control herself, yelled and ran out of the room. Then Mrs. Pidgeon turned back on me again, with more crazy accusations that I didn't quite understand.'

'How long did this go on?'

'Not for very long. I realized that she was being irrational, and it made no sense for me to even try to talk to her. I confess, I got a little indignant myself. I may have said something to the effect that I couldn't talk to her while she was in that kind of state. She must have taken it as disrespect because of how she reacted.'

'What did she do?'

'She started to yell some more. Then she stopped. She got really quiet, just simmering and glaring at me. It was kind of scary. Then she just abruptly said something like, 'I think your services are no longer needed here, Melinda. Gather your things and get out.' Something like that. And she shoved a handful of money at me. She just kept telling me to leave in that same quiet, scary voice. I started getting upset myself. Finally I left in kind of a huff. She got to me. It was all so stupid.' Melinda paused and wiped an eye. 'And that was the last time I ever saw her or spoke with her.' With self-conscious dignity, Melinda composed herself and looked at them expectantly.

'Ms. Barstow, we're going to need to take this letter with us.'

Melinda nodded. 'I figured that. If it can be of any help, you're welcome to it.'

'I'm afraid we also need the money. We'll give you a receipt. If it was actually sent to you by Jessica, you'll get it back.'

Melinda nodded again, this time with a resigned scowl on her face. 'I figured that too.'

'You could have neglected to tell us about it. You're an honest person. We appreciate that. It might have importance.'

Melinda rose from her chair and walked to a breakfront on the other side of the living room and opened a drawer, pulling out a packet of bills with a thick rubber band around them. She brought it back and placed it on the table next to the envelope. Jilly had a clear plastic bag ready to carefully deposit the money.

'Fingerprinting currency is not usually very effective,' she explained, 'but we have to give it a shot, along with some other tests the lab can do. We'll certainly fingerprint the letter. We'll need to exclude your own prints. Perhaps you could come to the station and get fingerprinted, unless you already have them on record?'

Melinda began to look more concerned. 'I was fingerprinted when I applied for my work visa here, and when I applied for citizenship.'

'Then we'll be able to get them to compare. You'll be in the system, most likely. Where did you come from?'

'The Bahamas, twelve years ago.' She

set her jaw and glared at Jilly. 'I'm a legal citizen. I obey the laws. And I had nothing to do with what happened to Mrs. Pidgeon! I didn't do anything! I'm being honest with you!'

Jilly shook her head and waved her hands gently. 'You aren't suspected of anything. But suppose this letter was written by someone other than Mrs. Pidgeon. Suppose it has something to do with how she died. We have to be able to eliminate her prints. And yours. That's all.'

Melinda still did not look convinced. Jilly rose from her seat and placed a hand on her shoulder. 'Listen to me, Ms. Barstow. We don't care what your work situation was, or your citizenship status. That's not our job here.' She took a breath and fastened a stony, resolute gaze upon her, forcing her to stare back attentively. 'You'll have to forgive me for being blunt. Your employer, Jessica Pidgeon, someone you've known for years, a small, slight woman, was brutally assaulted, apparently by someone much bigger and stronger than her. It continued even after she was killed. Then she was left in a garbage container, like so much refuse. Her last minutes of conscious life were spent experiencing a level of contempt and degradation no human being should ever have to undergo. The person who did this needs to be found and punished and we need your cooperation. That's all we care about. Nothing else matters right now except finding the, the ... *monster* who did this.'

A tear slowly formed and trickled down Melinda's cheek. She pursed her lips tightly and nodded.

4

'This adds a whole new side to things,' Dan was saying. They were sitting at a table in what was called the station's cafeteria, but which in reality was little more than a self-serve coffee stand, each nursing a cardboard-sleeved cup of hot black coffee. 'Considering the husband didn't tell us he wasn't living there anymore.'

'And hadn't been for some time,' Jilly added. 'He didn't feel a need to tell us they were estranged.'

'Sounds like we need to go back and have another talk with him. Melinda mentioned he had taken an apartment here in the city. Should be easy enough to track down an address.'

'Maybe he'll still be at the house. He had to bring his kids back from the mother-in-law. We need to go to the neighborhood to talk to Jessica's friends anyway. That would make it easier.'

The letter and the package of money had

been bagged and sent to SID, with hopes of pulling fingerprints. They had agreed to misgivings regarding the letter, the money, and the story. But they had also agreed that Melinda herself seemed a less likely suspect for the murder.

Before sending it off, Jilly had snapped pictures of the manila envelope in which the letter and the money had been mailed. It had been covered with stamps, of the self-sticking variety, that had been stuck down in haphazard fashion — considerably more postage than would have actually been required. The postmark, from a postal station only a few blocks from Jessica's ATM, indicated it had been processed on Monday morning. They decided that everything pointed to the strong possibility that the envelope had been prepared ahead of time. The money could have been inserted and the package sealed and dropped into a mailbox outside the station sometime on Sunday. A trip to the post office might or might not prove to be helpful — both Jilly and Dan tended to believe not — but they needed to try. It was a quick trip and as fruitless as they had expected. Nobody at the postal station recalled the parcel, nor could they offer any helpful information on how it might have been processed.

It was time to focus on more important objectives, fortunately at two adjacent destinations: another conversation with James Pidgeon and a visit to Dory Snyder up the street. On the drive to Farmington, they discussed the puzzling implications of the mail parcel.

'It could be as simple as Jessica feeling guilty, going to get cash, and sending it off to Melinda,' Dan was saying, once again sitting in the passenger side of the car as Jilly drove.

'But you don't think so, and neither do I.'

'Too much is too weird. But Jessica definitely withdrew that money.'

'It's got to be the same money,' continued Jilly. 'I'm hoping there'll be a different set of fingerprints on the letter, the money, the stamps ... something to implicate another party.'

'Is it possible Jessica did all this, then got robbed and killed after dropping the package in the mail?'

'Maybe. Every scenario I can think of

raises questions for me. Why withdraw cash on a Sunday night, and why from that bank? I bet that's not her normal branch and that there's one closer to her house. Why would she type a letter of apology that way, and why would she mail it all so far from her home in the dead of the night on that Sunday?'

'And then there's the matter of her signature,' Dan added. 'Using her original and married names.'

'That too. Why was she in the city that night to begin with? If she was robbed by Marmaduke or whoever, how did she get to be there?'

'Let's hope Mr. Pidgeon will provide us with some insights.' Dan sighed, looking out the window. 'Here we are, Coventry Drive.'

Jilly pulled up in front of the Pidgeon house. 'Dory Snyder lives four houses up the street.'

'Might be more efficient to split up, what do you think?'

'Sure. You want to take Dory?'

'I'll walk. I could use the exercise.'

* * *

The door was answered by a blonde girl, presumably Laurie Pidgeon. Jilly identified herself and asked to speak with her father. The girl inspected her badge and ID carefully before stepping back and letting her in. Smart girl, Jilly thought.

The girl was in the teenage uniform of the day, leggings and a long sweater. She gave Jilly a look up and down. The scowl on her face looked as if it had found a permanent home there. 'You don't look like a detective.'

Jilly smiled. 'What do you mean?'

'All the woman detectives on TV wear pantsuits. And they have their badges hooked on their belts.'

'I hope you're not disappointed, but in real life some of us wear blazers and jeans. And I only display my badge at crime scenes and things like that. You must be Laurie, right? You were in Pennsylvania with your grandmother?'

The girl nodded. 'My brother and I just got back this morning.'

'I'm very sorry about your mom, Laurie.'

'My mom can go to hell,' Laurie said sullenly. 'She's probably there now.'

That took Jilly aback. It was a few short beats before she could gather her wits, but by then Laurie had said, in the same tone of voice, 'I'll go get my dad. Have a seat,' and pointed to the chairs in the living room before bounding up the nearby staircase.

Jilly sat down in the same chair she had taken the day before and found herself lost in thought. Apparently the relationship between Jessica and her daughter had been rocky of late. Not unusual, she considered. Sixteen was usually a difficult age, for both parent and child. She well remembered being that age, trying to assert herself as an independent person, wanting to be an adult all at once, constantly at loggerheads with her own mother. Add in the traumatic death of Laurie's mom and she could understand that the girl might be confused and prone to inappropriate expression. Witnessing people dealing with grief was nothing new to Jilly. She knew it far better than she would have wanted.

'Detective, how may I help you?' James entered the room alone, looking haggard and distracted.

Jilly stood up to greet him. 'Mr. Pidgeon, I'm sorry to bother you but I have a few more questions.'

'Okay. Please, sit down.' They both sat, across from one another. He looked at Jilly and waited.

'I see your kids have returned. How are they doing through this?'

'Hard to say. Nobody's talking much.'

'And how are you doing?'

James shrugged. 'I think I'm still in shock. At some point it's all going to come crashing down on me, the reality of it. If it was just me it'd be one thing ...'

'I understand.' Jilly waited a beat before proceeding. 'Mr. Pidgeon, you said you were out of town on business all last weekend?'

That stopped him short. 'Yes. I was in Portland, from Friday until Monday morning. I was conferring with our prospective buyer, Ubertech. Willy Gauss, the owner, is an old friend and colleague.'

'And what airline did you fly back on Monday morning?'

Pidgeon drew a deep breath. 'Horizon

Air. I got in at about 10. Why?'

'Would you happen to have kept your ticket?'

'Yes. It's a digital ticket, on my phone.'

'I'd like to see it if I might.'

Pidgeon sighed deeply and reached in his pocket for his phone. He tapped around on it and handed it to Jilly. She made note of the information and handed the phone back to him.

'This is beginning to sound like I'm a suspect,' Pidgeon said cautiously.

'Mr. Pidgeon, you haven't been living here, have you? You've been living in the city for a while now, isn't that right?'

He sank his head very low. Jilly watched him carefully. He finally looked up again. His eyes looked weary. 'No, I haven't been living in here for a while now.'

'You and your wife were separated? You were having difficulties?'

'You could say that.'

'I find it curious that you didn't mention that to us when we were here yesterday.'

'I didn't really think about it, to tell you the truth. You'd just told me my wife had died ... that she'd been killed. I'd been worried out of my mind about her since she'd disappeared.'

'I really need for you to tell me about it now,' Jilly said. 'How long ago did you move out?'

'It was about five or six weeks ago.'

'Sounds like something rather serious between you.'

'I'd like to say we were working it out, but.... no, I don't think we were going to work it out.' Jilly decided to let that hang, see how the silence might move him to elaborate. Finally he spoke. 'Jessy was ... difficult. I just couldn't deal with her anymore.'

'How do you mean?'

'Nothing seemed to be able to make her happy anymore. She was uncommunicative ... when she wasn't finding fault with every-thing. Nothing I did was ever good enough. She said I worked too hard, was gone from the house too much. But then when I was home, it was always fault-finding.' James stared across at Jilly. 'I guess sometimes marriages just run out of steam. People change too much. I don't know.'

Jilly kept waiting. The silence seemed

uncomfortable to him. He had to fill it up.

'You have to understand, I still love her. I always loved her. I don't understand what happened to her. She got so unhappy. Someone once told me that's a good definition of neurotic: being incapable of ever being happy.'

'You think Jessica was neurotic? Was she seeing a therapist of any kind?'

'Oh yeah. She went to a couple of them. She gave up on them, didn't think they could help.'

'Why do you think she was unhappy?'

'You're asking was it something I did?'

'No, Mr. Pidgeon, I'm just trying to get an idea of Jessica's state of mind, to understand where she may have gone Sunday and why.'

'I don't know, Detective. I long since gave up on trying to understand Jessy, what made her tick. I hadn't been paying that much attention to her comings and goings because I wasn't here any more than I needed to be, to see the kids and such.'

Jilly looked up to make sure that neither of the kids were in hearing range.

'I have to ask this. Are you involved with

another woman?'

He hesitated, considering his answer. Finally he shrugged in resignation. 'It didn't start that way. When I moved out, that wasn't the reason. But now, yes.'

'Did Jessica know, or at least suspect?'

'She *suspected* all sorts of things. Most of them groundless. I hadn't gotten around to telling her yet. It wasn't easy to tell her anything any longer.'

'Does this woman live with you now?'

'Not exactly. We spend time with each other, but it hasn't gotten to the stage where one of us is willing to give up their own place. You're not going to have to bring her into this, are you?'

'We are going to have to talk to her, yes. I'll need to know her name and some contact information.'

He sighed. 'Her name's Natasha Hedgefield. She works for me.' Jilly had her notebook out and was jotting down the name, address and phone number he provided. James shook his head with a grimace. 'She's still doing it.'

'Excuse me?'

'Oh ... I'm sorry. It's just that Jessy is

still making trouble for me even now.' He ran a hand across the top of his forehead. 'Forgive me, that was a terrible thing to say. I might not sound like I still loved Jessy, but believe me, I did. Nothing in my life was a harder task these days.'

'Had your son and daughter been getting along with their mother okay lately? Did they ever confide to you about having problems with her?'

James sighed deeply. 'Brad's at that age where he doesn't communicate much. He mostly stays in his room when he's home. That's what he's been doing since he got back this morning. I guess that's how boys process something this awful. Of late he hasn't tended to tell me much anyway. He'd go quiet for long periods when he was with me, like he was brooding.'

'And Laurie?'

'Laurie had some feud going on with Jessy over a boyfriend, it seems. Jessy would go on rants about how inappropriate he was for her.'

'Inappropriate. Strange way to put it. Why? Did you ever meet the boy?'

'Sure, once or twice. He's in some

trade-technical program at school, I think he wants to be a mechanic or something. Jessy objected that he wasn't going to go to college.'

'I assume Laurie plans to do so?'

'I certainly hope so. She's a bright girl. She could have a great future. She's only just finishing her sophomore year in high school; we've talked about it a little.'

'And Jessica, I gather, really wanted Laurie to go on to college?'

'Oh my God yes. It was like it was a done deal, no debate.'

'So that might have been another bone of contention between them?'

'It was all one big bone. I think Jessy had Laurie's whole life planned out for her. It was like if she lived vicariously through Laurie, she might find the happiness she was missing out on in her own life.'

'Wow,' said Jilly. 'That's quite the observation, Mr. Pidgeon. It sounds like you've been thinking about this for a while.'

James nodded slowly, gazing at her with sad eyes. 'I've been trying to figure this out for a long time.'

'You said Jessica saw a couple of

therapists? Recently?'

'The more recent one was maybe a year and a half ago. She first saw a male therapist about three years back, but she gave up on him after two visits because she said he didn't understand her. She said only a woman could understand. So I urged her to find a woman. That's why she finally started seeing Claire Orzibal. She saw her regularly for about six months before she gave up on her as well.'

Jilly jotted down the name. 'What did you think of her?'

'I never met her. I just wrote the checks to her.'

'What did Jessica think of her?'

'At first she'd come home and say she thought Claire was helping her see things. That's how she put it, see things. She seemed hopeful. She seemed to like going to talk with her. Then after a few weeks all of a sudden her enthusiasm died and she started saying that Claire wasn't what she had thought after all. One day she just didn't make any more appointments and stopped going to see her.'

'What was Jessica's state of mind like

right after that?'

'She seemed to plunge back into her depression, or whatever it was that was wrong.'

'Was Jessica on any kind of medication? Did Dr. Orzibal prescribe anything, perhaps for depression?'

'Not that I know.'

'Is there any possibility that Jessica was, well, self-medicating; that there was a drug issue that might have caused her emotional problems?'

'I can't imagine that. Jessy hated to take drugs of any kind. She bought organic foods. It was a task to get her to take something for a headache.'

'Where would I find Dr. Orzibal?'

'Her office and practice are in the city. I can probably find her information but I'm sorry, Jessy moved everything around after I left and I'd have to dig through her records.'

'I can likely find her easy enough. If not, I'll get back to you.'

'Do you honestly think Dr. Orzibal can give you any clue as to what happened to Jessy?'

It was Jilly's turn to sigh deeply. 'I don't

know, Mr. Pidgeon. I have to try. Frankly, Jessica is still a total enigma to me. I've got no idea where the insight is going to come from. I'm going to try everything I can, until the answers come.'

'I notice you don't say *if* the answers come. You expect them to come.'

'I'm not one to give up.' She eyed him levelly. 'And in the end I guess I'm an optimist.'

James nodded, lapsing into awkward silence before Jilly resumed.

'She made a withdrawal of money from the ATM at the Continental Interbank branch on Scully Boulevard on Sunday night. Is that something out of the ordinary for her?'

'Scully Boulevard? Yes, that's very unusual. I didn't even know there was a branch there. Continental's our bank, but she would have been more likely to use the branch at Farmington Plaza. That's a mall not far from here. A couple of her favorite stores are there. You say she took out money?'

'Yes. Four hundred dollars. There's a video of her making the transaction on

Sunday night.'

'Why would she do that?'

'I was hoping you could tell me.'

'Scully Boulevard, in the city?'

'Yes, sir.'

'I can't even think of anything around there that would have been of interest to her. Lately she hated to drive into the city. She wanted to stay here in Farmington. She even avoided driving, as much as possible. As far as I know, she only drove to the club and to the mall. And probably to the market and the kids' schools since she fired Melinda.'

'What market did she use?'

'I don't know. I'd guess the Esplanade, near the Plaza. Nice organic food market. Jessy tried to eat healthy. She had a thing about the whole family eating healthy.'

Jilly made a quick note. Jessica had to have gone somewhere last weekend. She was willing to grasp at straws.

* * *

Dan had stepped up to the stuccoed portico and had barely pressed the doorbell when the round-topped door flew open and a small woman with ashen hair and large eyeglasses gazed up at him. He had his badge and ID out to show her.

'You must be the detective!' she exclaimed, pulling open the door. 'I thought you were going to be a woman! Come in!' She was wearing a smock and had one armful of rocks that looked like pieces of granite. She stepped back to let him in.

'Give me a moment!' she said excitedly. 'I've been collecting these rocks for my garden, let me go put them down!' She scurried out towards the back of the house. Dan looked around uncomfortably. He heard a screen door in the back of the house creak and slam, then a few seconds later it creaked and slammed again. The little woman returned the way she had left, now minus smock or rocks.

'I'm sorry. I spent this morning finding those beautiful rocks up in the hills. They're for my garden.'

'Yes, ma'am,' Dan replied. 'What kind of garden do you have?'

'Why, a rock garden, of course! Come in, please, sit down!' She led him into a

high-ceilinged living room sparely deco-
rated in southwest style: earth tones, numerous terra cotta pots, a woven wall hang.
They both sat on short burnt-orange sofas
that faced one another across a low coffee
table bearing a few ceramic figurines. She
started fingering the turquoise stones of a
large chunky necklace she wore.

'I heard about poor Jessica! What a terrible
thing!' The woman had enormous energy, it
seemed to Dan. She sat but never stopped
fidgeting. When she stopped playing with the
necklace, she began to move items around
on the coffee table. She adjusted her shirt.
'That's why you're here, isn't it? I spoke to
a young woman earlier ...'

'That would be my partner, Jilly Garvey.
Yes, Ma'am.'

'I haven't had the chance to go over to
see her family. Those poor children! I'll have
to see if I can do anything for them!'

'I understand you were close to Mrs.
Pidgeon.'

'Well, I don't know if 'close' is the right
word. Certainly we knew one another. And
we often met for coffee or sometimes lunch.
At least, we used to.'

'You hadn't seen her much recently?'

'Not very recently, I'm afraid. Jessica seemed to prefer keeping her own counsel of late.'

'I don't understand. You mean she just decided not talk to you anymore?'

'Not exactly.' Dory hesitated, looking uncomfortable. 'It was getting awkward in recent times. She was ... aggravated. Frankly, it was hard to talk to her. She was argumentative and testy. Yes, that's a good word for it. Jessica had gotten very testy.'

'Do you know why she might have gotten like that?'

'It could have been a number of things. She complained about her children and her family and her life. She said she felt everything was out of control.'

'So ... you decided to sever connections with her?'

'It was more like I thought I'd give her some time to get things together, become herself again. It was just too hard. Perhaps in a while, things would be back to normal again.'

'How long ago did this happen? When

did you stop getting together with her?'

'I don't know; it was a few weeks ago. I just stopped calling her and figured if she called me, I'd make some excuses for a while. As it turns out, I didn't need to. After a couple of weeks I realized she wasn't calling me anymore either.'

'Did you wonder if there was something specific troubling her? Did you ever ask her?'

'Oh, of course. Many times. She always dismissed my questions and said there was nothing in particular.' She looked up earnestly at Dan. 'You have to understand something, Mr. Lee. Jessica was my friend. We were close for a long time. She was possibly my best friend in this neighborhood, especially since my husband died a while back.'

'I'm sorry,' Dan interjected.

'Thank you. He fought a long protracted illness. It was very hard. Jessica was there for me through it and afterward. My point is that I would have done anything to help her if I could. If she would have let me. But she wouldn't let me in. She wouldn't tell me what was the matter.'

'Do you think she confided to anybody else? Family, friends?'

'Family?' Dory expelled air through her lips. 'Her husband, you mean? I don't think he was there for her very much. She has no other family nearby, at least that I know of. Her mother lives somewhere back east. Delaware or Pennsylvania if I recall.'

'Pennsylvania, yes. How about other friends?'

'She didn't seem to have a lot of close friends in the area. She and her husband were cordial enough. There were outdoor barbecues and parties and such. But close friends? Over time she seemed to drop out of the social circuit. There was me and sometimes a couple of friends she met at the club.'

'The country club?'

'Yes, I suppose you could call it that. The Cypress Golf and Tennis Club. Jessica liked to play tennis and swim. We'd sometimes meet her to play cards or just sit by the pool and have a glass of wine.' She smiled a little. 'Or two.'

'Besides you, who else would she socialize with?'

'Well, Tamara. She and Jessica seemed to have little conspiracies they would laugh about.'

'Tamara ...?'

'Marsh, I believe is her last name. When we'd play bridge, which wasn't that often, we'd get someone for a fourth. But mostly it was the three of us. I once joked we were the Three Musketeers. Tamara said no, it was more like the Unholy Three.'

'That's interesting. Tamara sounds like she's a bit of a sharp wit.'

'Oh, yes. She likes to say her patron saint is Dorothy Parker.'

'So the three of you got along well, and sometimes there'd be a fourth, but nobody regular?'

'No. Nobody ever stuck, you might say.'

'Would you know how I could contact Tamara?'

'Tamara lives further up in the hills. Her husband's name is Paul, I think. She mentioned him on occasion. That's all I know. He was always off playing golf. He's a fanatic. But I guess all the husbands are. I don't know anyone who ever just dabbled in golf, do you?'

'Never played it, so I really couldn't say. Mr. Pidgeon never joined the golf games?'

'Oh no. He hasn't set foot in the club in a long time. Only Jessica.'

'Do you think they were still close in recent weeks, when Jessica became more, well, distracted?'

Dory shrugged. 'I don't know. Couldn't tell by me. I'm out of the loop now.' She suddenly looked a bit put out.

'So you haven't seen them at the club recently?'

'Oh, I'm not a member. I was always Jessica's guest there. I guess I'm not much of a mixer. Especially since my husband passed.' A furry white cat strolled into the room and leapt into her lap, and she idly stroked it, staring sadly into space. 'I'm kind of a loner of late. Just me. And Tabitha here. And my garden.'

The ensuing silence grew awkward for Dan. He strained for something to break it. 'Your rock garden.'

'Yes. I guess I miss having Jessica come to visit. Oh my. And now I'll never see her again.'

Dan tried to bring the conversation back

in focus. 'Do you know of any other friends at all that Jessica might have had? Any other hobbies, activities? Did she go out much, go shopping or horseback riding or anything you can think of?'

'She did things mostly on her own. She liked shopping for clothes but she hated going into the city. She'd mostly go to the malls. She liked a couple of the nicer stores out at Farmington Plaza. That was what you'd call her comfort zone.'

'What was Jessica's marriage and family life like?'

'I couldn't really tell you. When Dion — that was my husband — was alive, we'd socialize with the Pidgeons. But since he died, I can't recall seeing the both of them together. There was only Jessica. I think Mr. Pidgeon was like me, no great desire to mingle.'

'She must have talked about it, though. Her marriage, I mean.'

Dory's smile was deeply sad. 'I don't think she was very happy. She would say strange things about nobody liking her or listening to her. But I honestly don't know if that was her marriage and her family, or …'

'Yes? Or?'

Dory looked as if she were trying to solve a difficult puzzle. '... or if it was just her, if her sense of reality was warping. I really began to think something was wrong with her.'

★ ★ ★

The conversation with James Pidgeon continued to be comfortable enough but yielded little insight for Jilly. He seemed willing to talk about everything but seemed to know almost nothing. It seemed he had long since become emotionally removed from his wife, and to only a slightly lesser extent from his children.

'Mr. Pidgeon,' Jilly asked, 'did Jessica keep any kind of journal? Anything that might give us a clue what she was doing this past weekend?'

'I'd guess not. At least she never did when I was here. She wasn't one to be all that introspective, if you know what I mean.'

'Did she write letters to people?'

'You mean, like actual letters? Maybe a thank-you card now and then. Some polite

115

acknowledgment. She was fairly proper about that kind of thing.'

'Did she have any kind of stationery to use if she did write a letter? Or would she have just written it up on her computer and printed it out?'

'I'm not sure, Detective. What are you getting at?'

'She sent a letter to Melinda. And she included the letter of recommendation Melinda needed. Everything was typed in a word processing program and printed out on plain paper, and mailed in a plain manila envelope. Would she have done that from her computer here?'

'She wrote a long letter and *mailed* it to Melinda? I don't know. That strikes me as kind of strange.'

'Can I see her office or wherever she might have worked from?'

'Probably the bedroom. Follow me.' They rose and he led Jilly up the stairway. At the landing, they walked down a short corridor and James opened a door to a large bedroom. 'This used to be ours, but it's been Jessy's room since I left. I couldn't bring myself to sleep in here the past few days. I'm in the guest room down the hall.'

Near the bed there was a desk with a small computer and printer. James gestured toward it and said, 'Feel free to look. I'm going to go call Jessy's mother. I forgot to let her know the kids arrived safely. I'll only be a moment.'

'Of course.'

Jilly pulled on a pair of her ever-present latex gloves from her pocket and opened each drawer, carefully leafing through its contents. Each drawer was sparsely filled and neatly arranged. She found two boxes of pastel stationery and small envelopes, but no postage stamps. There were no large manila envelopes, not even a package of plain printing paper. The wide shallow drawer over the kneehole of the desk contained a few pencils and ballpoint pens and a small notepad. Jilly inspected the pad to see if there were any impressions from previous writing on a top sheet, but it seemed to be fresh. She tried out each of the pens on the pad. Two were black and one was red. No blue. No felt tips. The computer and printer were turned off. When she turned them on, there was no password needed to access the screen. A quick perusal yielded no recently created documents or files of any kind, and certainly no evidence of having written a letter or recommendation.

It would appear that Jessica had not composed the letter on this machine, unless she had then scrupulously removed every trace. Jilly doubted it since the trash file on the screen was full, with items dating back over two weeks. There were three sheets of standard size paper in the printer, but they were a light buff color, not white like the letter had been.

She sat quietly and took stock. They should get an evidence team up here in any case. There might be some ...

She heard the slight noises behind her, from the doorway. Not much more than a foot shuffling on the hall carpet.

'Laurie, if that's you, it's okay, you can come out.'

The girl slowly entered, looking guilty, sullen and wary. 'I heard you and my father talking down there.'

'How long were you listening?'

'A while.'

'I'm sorry about what you might have

heard. We were hoping to keep this private.'

'I'm not a kid.' Laurie sat tentatively on the edge of her mother's bed, staring down at her hands in her lap.

'This has to be awful for you. Maybe you shouldn't subject yourself to all this.'

'I hate her,' Laurie said quietly.

'Your mom? This must just be shock talking.'

'No. I hate her. I'm glad she's dead.'

'Laurie, I don't think you really mean that. I guess you know how your mother died.' The girl nodded. 'Nobody should die that way.'

'I don't care.'

'You're angry right now.'

'No kidding. You really are a detective.'

'Can I ask you what she did to make you so angry?'

'She tried to run my life. She just wanted me to be as unhappy as she was. She wanted everybody to be as unhappy as her.'

'Why do you think she was so unhappy?'

'I don't know. It's stupid. She had everything. She could do whatever she wanted, go wherever she pleased, and she never wanted to do anything. She hated us all.'

'And what did she do to you in particular?'

'She wouldn't let me grow up. She dictated my life, even what I ate. She ruined everything good that happened to me. If I liked it, it was bad.'

'I don't understand when you say she wouldn't let you grow up. I get the impression she was proud that were a good student and would be going to college —'

'That's what *she* wanted! I don't want to go to college! She suspected me of being a ... a ... just a really bad person. She thought my friends were evil.'

'Evil. That's a heavy word. She disapproved of your friends?'

'She wanted me to hang out with the girls *she* liked at my school. Which is pathetic since she never had anything to do with the schools we go to anymore. She never came around or talked with the parents or the teachers anymore.'

'You clearly didn't share your mother's opinion of the girls she did approve of.'

Laurie almost spat. 'They're a bunch of minions.'

'Minions?'

'You know. Lackeys. Ass-kissers. They say all the right things to the adults. They have all the parents fooled that they're sweet, smart and lovable. Actually they're elitist bullies. They act totally different when the parents and teachers aren't around. I hate them. And they hate me. They make life miserable for everybody who doesn't fit into their little clique.'

'And the kids you like to hang out with ...?'

'My friends are nice people! They're not cool, they're not trendies. They're just good solid people. All she could see was that they were different. And a lot of them aren't on the academic track. They're not the *right* people.'

'Do you have a boyfriend like that too? Was that an issue?'

'He's not really my boyfriend. He's a friend. A good friend. He's smart and sweet and honest. She hates him. Hated him, I mean. All she could see was that he's not going to college. He wants to work on cars. What's wrong with that? She said he was nasty and a gangbanger. Like she'd even know what a gangbanger was like. She had some other names for him too. She thought he was 'taking advantage' of me and gave me this lecture about what 'that kind of boy' is like. As if she had any idea. Actually the guys she liked at my school are a lot more like that. All the socials are like that. They're disrespectful. They treat girls terribly.'

'Your ... your friend. What's his name?'

'Robbie. That's short for Roberto. Get the picture?'

Jilly sighed. She was getting it all too well.

'Laurie, did all of this have anything to do with Melinda getting fired?'

'Laurie! What are you doing here?' James had returned to the bedroom, still holding a cordless phone in his hand.

Laurie jumped to her feet. 'I'm just leaving.'

'Wait, Laurie,' said Jilly, also rising to her feet. She pulled a business card out of the pocket of her blazer. 'Here's my card, with both my numbers on it. Call me any time if you'd like to just talk with someone, okay?'

Laurie hesitated but took the card, then turned on her heel and ran out of the room.

'What was all that about?' asked James. 'Has she been listening? Did she hear us talking?'

'I think so. How much does she know about how her mother died?'

'I tried to spare her the details. Of course she's going to hear things. I can't totally protect her. But I didn't think she needed to know ...'

'I understand. This is coming down on her awfully hard. You're going to have to be very patient with her. She's going to say a lot of things that might shock you.'

'Yeah. I'm already getting that. When she's not giving me the silent treatment.'

'Whether or not she shows it, she needs you very much right now. So does your son. Be there for them. If Laurie feels more comfortable talking to a woman, I'll be glad to sit down and listen.'

Jilly decided, being on her feet already, that it was time to end the visit. She had covered everything that she could for the moment. 'Thank you for your time. We'll probably need to do a closer inspection of Jessica's things. I'll need you to close off this room. We may need to process some other areas as well. I'll be in touch shortly with more details.'

'That's easy. I don't want to be in this

house at all. Too many memories. I pretty much stick to the guest room and the kitchen and living room. The kids stay in their rooms for the most part.'

'Mr. Pidgeon, before I leave, one more question.'

'Yes?'

'Did your wife ever use her family name, Carpenter?'

James gave Jilly a curious look. 'Not really. She went by Jessica Pidgeon ever since we were married. Why?'

'So she wasn't in the habit of signing her name, say, Jessica Carpenter or Jessica Carpenter Pidgeon?'

'No. I never saw her do that.'

'But Carpenter was her family name, wasn't it?'

'Yes. Why?'

'That's how she signed the letter she sent to Melinda.'

'Maybe on some formal document somewhere she might have done that, if it required her full name, like on our bank accounts or tax forms. But I can't remember ever seeing her use that in a signature.'

Jilly's phone buzzed. She excused herself

and checked it. A text message from Dan: he was finished, should he meet her at the Pidgeon house? She texted back a quick yes, adding to meet her out front at the car. She turned back to James.

'I'm sorry I had to bother you. We might be back in touch as questions arise or we get new information. Please contact me or Detective Lee if you think of anything else that might help us.'

'Of course. Oh … I got a call this morning. My wife will be available for burial in a day or two. I guess the autopsy is finished.'

Jilly nodded. 'Yes, it is.'

'I can plan the service now. Her mother's flying in tomorrow.'

'Are there other relatives?'

'Not really. Her mom's a widow. Jessy has no brothers or sisters, no cousins. Nobody she's been close with in years. She was even kind of sporadic with her mother. That was one reason she decided to send the kids to visit, actually took them out of school for a week. She hoped it would bring them closer together.' He shook his head. 'You're still looking at me, I'd guess.'

'Sir? Looking at you?'

'Isn't that the way you express it? I've heard that the spouse is the number one suspect. I find it hard to believe I'd be an exception.'

'Mr. Pidgeon, we're looking at everybody and everything right now. We're still trying to establish the facts, exactly what happened.'

James shrugged slightly. 'I wouldn't blame you. I have to admit, I must not look like the most loving partner in the world right now, do I? I'd probably be suspicious of me too.'

'That's a very strange thing to say, sir.'

James spread his hands in front of him. 'I don't understand it. I loved Jessy. This horrible thing has happened to her, but I still don't feel anything. I'm just numb.' He looked with confusion at Jilly. 'For a while now I was thinking that she was no longer the woman I knew and loved. Maybe in my heart I had mourned her loss already. I don't know.'

Jilly wasn't sure how to reply to that.

'Detective, I am not capable of doing something like this. I can't even comprehend how someone could have done something like this. Or why.'

She said her goodbyes and left him standing there in the living room.

5

By the time Jilly was on the walkway heading for the street, Dan was already waiting by the car.

'How'd it go with Dory?' Jilly asked.

'I don't know that she was all that helpful. She's kind of a ditz. But she mentioned Tamara Marsh at the country club. I recall the husband mentioned her as well. She might be of more help.'

Jilly consulted her watch. 'We've got time. We should drive over there.'

'Sounds good,' agreed Dan. 'While we're here, why not also take a minute and ask the next door neighbors a question or two. Just in case anybody saw her or spoke with her recently.'

'Good idea, partner. Which do you want, right or left?'

They both came up empty. There were neighbors at home to either side of the Pidgeon residence, but nobody in either house had even seen Jessica in several weeks, much less talked with her. It was as if a ghost had resided there. It became evident that it would be futile to take up any more time further up and down the block.

'So much for that,' sighed Dan as they returned to the car.

'Back to our plan,' Jilly said resignedly. 'The country club. And there's the matter of Jessica's therapist, in the city. Maybe she's not too far and it'll be worth taking a spin by.' She held up the car keys. 'Okay, come on, it's your turn. You drive, I'll ride and we can trade notes.'

Dan stood still. 'I'd rather you drove, if it's all the same.'

'Okay, look, enough of this. What is going on here, Dan?'

'What do you mean, what's going on?'

She rested her hands on her hips and glared in frustration. 'As somebody else just reminded me, I'm a detective, remember? I kind of noticed you haven't wanted to drive in a few days now. You usually like to do the driving or go off on your own. That's what I mean. What's going on, already?'

Dan chewed his lip pensively. Jilly waited, partly annoyed and, despite herself, partly amused.

'This is embarrassing,' he finally said.

'What? Come on. *What?*'

He spat it out like one of their perps confessing. 'I let my driver's license expire.'

It sunk in and then Jilly couldn't help herself. She exploded in laughter. She bent over, right there on the sidewalk, trying to contain herself. Dan watched her, red-faced, as she regained control, straightened up, and looked at him, wiping an eye. She was still smiling. 'You *what*?'

'I ... let my driver's license expire. I can't drive. Not legally.'

'Are you kidding?'

'We've just been so busy, it got by me. I mean, you can renew your car registration online, but you have to actually go into the Department of Motor Vehicles to renew your driver's license. I just sorta forgot.'

'How long ago did it expire?'

'On the weekend.'

There were undoubtedly numerous members of their unit that wouldn't have been discouraged from driving by a mere formality like a lapsed license. She suspected one guy in particular, Detective

Morrison by name, had been driving without a license for years now, based on his driving skills. Dan, Jilly reflected, was one of those straight arrows who played it by the book. He would go to extraordinary lengths to not break the law.

Jilly juggled the car keys, trying to suppress her laughter. 'Okay, so I guess I'm driving until you get to the DMV then.'

'I made an appointment but the earliest I could get was tomorrow afternoon. I could have just walked in but I could end up waiting in line for hours and hours, and I don't have that kind of time. This case is just taking up so much. As it is, it's going to take me away for too long.'

'Dan, I'll cover you. We have to get you back behind the wheel, partner, before you forget how to drive altogether.' She walked around to the driver's side and opened the door. 'Do me a favor and get on your phone GPS and navigate us to the Cypress Golf and Tennis Club, will you?'

She was still smiling and Dan was still blushing as they drove away from the curb. 'What's your feeling on the husband?' Dan asked.

Jilly shook her head. 'He's a piece of work. Talk about self-absorbed. Pretty much withdrawn from the family. He and Jessica weren't getting along. And there is a girlfriend in the picture.'

'Are you liking him for this?'

'I'm not getting that feeling. As I said, he's kind of wrapped up in himself, but he seems genuinely shaken. And he's got a possible alibi from Friday through Monday morning. But we've got to look at him, as he put it himself. I'll check with the company he says he was visiting in Portland, and with the airline. But if that pans out, then he wasn't here when she was killed.'

'If he was away, any possibility of an arrangement? Maybe he's the link to Marmaduke, a murder-for-hire?'

Jilly shook her head. 'That seems a long shot. Marmaduke doesn't strike me as the kind of guy you'd hire to mow your lawn, much less pull off a clean murder.'

'Yeah, but Pidgeon doesn't strike me as the kind of guy who'd have any connections with anybody more professional.'

'Let's see how the rest of the facts fall.'

'So we're back to Jessica,' mused Dan.

'Trying to figure out what she was doing that weekend and why. And that whole business with the money and the letter. There's so much that's strange about that.'

'It appears that nobody saw or spoke with her for the entire weekend before she died,' Jilly said. 'The kids, and let's assume the husband, were gone Friday. She didn't talk with any of her neighbors, not even her friend Dory. She'd stopped seeing the therapist and she didn't tend to go out. None of the credit cards we recovered had been used over the weekend. It was like she was a hermit.'

'Maybe this Tamara talked with her.'

'Let's hope. I'm also thinking we should ask at the stores she frequented at that Farmington Plaza. Maybe she was there and somebody might remember her.'

'Not that far from the club; we can swing by there afterward.'

'And Claire Orzibal might be of help. Jessica seems to have been troubled lately. She wasn't opening up to anybody around her.'

Dan had his smart phone in hand and was accessing his internet connection. 'I'll look her up and give her a call, find out how soon we can see her.'

Jilly muttered half to herself, 'And I really want to talk to that girlfriend, Natasha.'

Dan looked up. 'Natasha? Really? Sounds exotic.'

'We've got to get some clue to Jessica's state of mind and where she might have gone. I don't think any of this case is going to make any sense until we do.'

Dan had found a phone number and dialed it. He had a short conversation and tapped the connection off. 'Dr. Orzibal is right over the city line. She can see us later today, after her last patient. We've got about four hours.'

'Let's make the best of it.'

★   ★   ★

They lucked out at the country club. The manager was quite cooperative and he said that the Marshes were present. Mr. Marsh was with a golf foursome and Mrs. Marsh could be found on the pool patio. He directed them out to poolside, which only had a few people scattered about, sitting at

134

tables and talking. They had little problem picking out Tamara Marsh instantly, sitting by herself at a table under a large umbrella. She was a bony, long-haired brunette with oversized sunglasses and a tall cocktail glass in front of her. She pulled down her sunglasses to gaze at them as they approached. Jilly introduced them and showed her ID.

'Oh my God,' Tamara drawled. Her voice was deep and smoky and it was clear she was not on her first cocktail. 'This is about Jessica, isn't it? It has to be about Jessica.'

'Yes, I'm afraid so. May we sit down?'

Tamara waved a hand as if it didn't matter to her if they sat or stood. They pulled out chairs. A waiter in black shirt and pants materialized, seemingly out of thin air, and asked if he could bring them anything. They both shook their heads and he vanished as magically as he had appeared.

'I heard the news only this morning,' Tamara said. 'It's so terrible. She was killed in a robbery or something like that?' Her words and demeanor didn't match well. She spoke levelly without emotion, though with a discernible effort to form her words.

'That's what we're trying to figure out.

We hoped you might be able to help us. When was the last time you spoke with Jessica?'

'Let's see. It was sometime last week. She came by the club a couple of times. Wednesday. A week ago today.'

'And you haven't talked, on the phone perhaps, or had any word from her since last Wednesday?'

'We seldom talk on the phone. Mostly we get together here. Jessica likes to swim and sometimes to play tennis. I guess I should say she liked to do those things.' She regarded Jilly through her dark lenses. 'This is so terrible. Poor little Jess.'

'What did you talk about the last time you saw her?'

'She was pretty flustered. She was trying to get her kids ready to go visit her mother. She lives somewhere in the east. She was frustrated.' Pronouncing the word presented some difficulty for her. She picked up her drink and took a long sip. 'Now she had to get them ready herself since she'd just fired her housekeeper. She said it was like trying to herd wild cattle lately, her kids all unmanageable — and now all this on top of everything else.'

'What did she mean by 'everything else'?' Jilly asked.

'They're teenagers. She said they were one hundred percent attitude. I suppose you know her husband had been gone for a while. It was just her and the housekeeper against the world — well, the world according to Jess. And now the housekeeper was out of the picture.'

'That would be Melinda Barstow we're talking about.'

Tamara nodded and took another long sip before putting the glass down on the table. She rolled the name out slowly. 'Me-lin-da. Uh-huh. I don't know her last name. I was surprised she'd been fired. She was with Jess a long time; she sounded quite capable. Believe me, it's not easy to find a good housekeeper.'

'I'm sure it's not. So the firing was rather abrupt?'

'Oh yes. It was the first I heard of any trouble with her.'

'So … why did she say she'd fired Melinda?'

'It seems she went behind Jess's back.

She was conspiring with the daughter.'

'Conspiring? Is that what she called it?'

'Her word precisely. Jess was ... prone to dramatics.' Tamara smiled impenetrably, her eyelids heavy. Jilly shot a look at her partner, who was watching Tamara with a strange expression of his own. 'The daughter was running with some crowd she did not approve of. Seems there was a boyfriend, too. They were all putting ideas in her head, according to Jess.'

'Ideas. Like what?' Jilly asked.

Tamara shrugged. 'To be honest, they sounded like pretty normal teenaged kids to me. Normal teenage is plenty scary enough. Do you have any kids, Detective?'

'No. Neither of us do.'

'If you ask me, Jess was just scared by the prospect of her kids growing up. Becoming independent. Challenging her. Maybe experimenting with things. I remember my own teenage years. It wasn't that long ago.' She smiled more deeply. 'Which reminds me. Damn, I wish they'd let us smoke out here.'

'Some specific incident seems to have precipitated the firing. Any idea what it might have been?'

'Jess said she'd gone out and came back to find out the housekeeper had brought her daughter home from school.' Now Tamara's voice turned dramatic as she warned to the juicy tale. 'Not only the daughter but also the forbidden boyfriend. They were up in the daughter's room! Apparently Jess had told the housekeeper that she wasn't going to be back for a while.'

'So she returned home unexpectedly. Laurie, the daughter, is up in her room with the boyfriend.'

'And the housekeeper is downstairs in the kitchen, clearly aware of the situation, and acting as if nothing in the world was wrong!'

'Did Jessica find them, well, doing anything?'

Tamara laughed. 'That was unclear. Jess was into such a rant by that stage of the story. My impression is, no, they were just sitting on the daughter's bed and talking. But he wasn't supposed to be in the house or anywhere near the daughter. And the housekeeper knew it.'

Jilly traded a long look with Dan.

'Jess called it a total betrayal,' Tamara continued smokily, her voice lapsing back into a kind of low crackle. Recently, Jilly mused, social commentators had begun to call that a 'vocal fry,' that popular throaty effect that some seemed to find sensual but many were finding tedious. 'She fired the gal on the spot; told her to get out and don't come back. It must have been some scene with the daughter as well. She described a screaming match after she chased the boyfriend out of the house.'

Dan spoke up. 'You seem to think she blew the whole thing out of proportion, though?'

Tamara turned to look at Dan for the first time since they sat down, as if she hadn't been aware of his being there. 'He speaks!' Dan actually flushed a little. Now she addressed them both. 'She was doing a lot of that lately. Blowing things out of proportion. For all I know, her story was totally delusional. I was getting worried about her.'

'How do you mean?'

'One of the things I've always loved about Jess is that we shared a kind of healthy cynicism, you know? There were a few of us who hung out poolside here and dished while our husbands did whatever they did, played golf or worked. We loved to deconstruct everything and everybody. It was kind of good naughty fun. But lately it wasn't so much fun anymore. Jess had turned a dark corner. She complained. I mean, her complaints were different. We weren't co-conspirators anymore. One by one the rest of the gang dropped out, and I think it was because of her.'

'Did Jessica talk about her husband much lately?' Dan asked.

'Just to complain. He was remote and distant, he didn't interact with the kids, he'd stopped being close to her, yadda yadda. And they fought about money.'

'Money? Anything specific?'

'Her husband started his own company, some kind of computer thing. She said for all the time he spent away from home, there wasn't much money to show for it. She began to figure he had a girlfriend, and that was where the time and the money were really going. That must have made for some hellacious arguments.'

'Did she have any proof that there was another woman?'

Tamara had picked up her drink once again, and it sloshed as she made a gesture with both hands. 'As I said, she was into drama. I don't know where the reality ended and the delusions began. All I know is the proportion of delusion just kept growing.'

★　★　★

'You're pretty quiet,' Jilly said as they pulled away from the country club's front drive. 'What are you thinking about all this?'

'I'm thinking she had a real bunch of winners in her life,' said Dan. 'Friends, family. My God.'

Jilly nodded grimly. 'I see your point.'

'We've got time before Dr. Orzibal can see us. Want to spin over to the mall and see if anybody remembers her in the stores she frequented?'

'Sounds like a plan. It's only about a mile away. She had credit cards for two stores over there. We can split up, show her picture. Maybe we'll get lucky. Maybe she was in there last weekend.'

Almost two hours later, they had not gotten lucky. Dan and Jilly had each taken one of the department stores to which Jessica seemed partial and questioned numerous salespeople and managers. In each case two people remembered Jessica by face as a customer (and others quickly recognized her as the recently killed woman in the news) but nobody could remember having seen her in at least a week. She had apparently not been shopping at those stores the weekend she disappeared. Their mutual disappointment was clear to each of them when they rendezvoused back in the parking lot.

They still had a few minutes so Jilly suggested the Esplanade market nearby. They had the same results: a couple of employees who recognized her, but nobody who recalled seeing her in the past week. Once again they returned to their car discouraged.

'Let's hope for something encouraging or insightful from Claire Orzibal,' Jilly sighed as she started up the ignition. 'Give me that address again, would you?'

* * *

Dr. Claire Orzibal was a short, alert-looking woman with short dark hair, and deep brown eyes behind stylish glasses. She was waiting for them in her reception room and introductions were made. She invited the detectives into her office, where she had already arranged chairs facing a sofa.

'Are you okay with our sitting here instead of around my desk?' she asked, with the slightest trace of an elusive accent. 'This just seems more comfortable.'

'This is fine, Doctor,' said Jilly. 'Thanks for seeing us on short notice.'

'Of course.' They sat on the chairs and Orzibal took the sofa. 'I was horrified by the news about Jessica. What a terrible thing. Do you know what exactly happened?'

'We were hoping you might help us figure out some of that,' said Dan.

Orzibal nodded gravely. 'I've considered ethical responsibilities here in terms of patient confidentiality and even sought advice from a couple of my colleagues. There are details I prefer not to divulge if they affect others, but in general, I'm comfortable having this conversation. Jessica is no longer alive, and I also want to see

144

justice done for her.'

'Forgive me if I take notes,' Dan continued, his notebook already in hand. Orzibal nodded. 'How long ago were you seeing her, and for how long?'

'She first started meeting with me a little less than two years ago. We had fairly regular sessions for about six months.'

'How often would you meet in that time?'

'We started once a week, then twice a week. For the last couple of months, she had again dropped back to once a week.'

Jilly picked up the questioning. 'Why was she seeing you, Doctor? What was the problem?'

Orzibal smiled. 'That's a complicated question, Detective Garvey. I suppose the easiest way to express it to you is that she was profoundly unhappy. We were trying to get to the root of that.'

'She'd seen a therapist before you, I understand.'

'Yes, a colleague of mine, a very capable man. He in fact referred her to me. She told me she didn't feel comfortable talking with a man, that she preferred to talk with another woman. That's not unusual.'

'Was this ... profound unhappiness ... something that had just come upon her relatively recently?'

'According to her, yes. She said that she increasingly felt that life had become overwhelming, uncontrollable. She often used that expression, that she felt out of control. She thought people were abandoning her. She felt unloved and unappreciated.'

'Were your sessions helping, do you think?'

Orzibal heaved a heavy sigh. 'My feeling was that Jessica suffered from severe chronic depression. I felt she needed more. I suggested medication, as well as proceeding with more intensive cognitive therapy.'

'Cognitive,' interjected Dan, 'meaning talking it out, digging up the root causes?'

'An interesting way to put it. Yes, more or less.'

'Did she agree to go on the medication?' Jilly asked.

'Not at first. She said she didn't think there was anything 'wrong' with her, that she mostly had to learn how to cope with everybody else, that they were the cause of her problems. That's not an unusual place to begin.'

'It sounds as if she resisted the cognitive therapy as well,' observed Dan.

'It takes time. She and I got off to a pretty good start. I think she genuinely liked me. More importantly, she began to trust me. Gradually she began to open up in our sessions. That's when we expanded to twice weekly.'

'Did she ever agree to medication?' asked Jilly.

'She finally decided to try something and we began with an antidepressant. After a week she said it made her feel funny and she wanted to stop. We tried a different one, with the same results. Jessica did not like drugs. She didn't even like taking aspirin or Tylenol.'

'Do you think you were making any headway?'

'Given more time, we would have. It's a slow process.'

'Then she cut back her visits and ultimately stopped coming?'

'Yes. That was her choice. She said she decided that this was not the answer.'

Orzibal looked deeply saddened.

'Do you think you could have turned her around if she'd kept coming?' Dan asked.

'It wouldn't have been me; it would have been she who might have turned *herself* around. With time, I thought she could have.'

'But you definitely think she needed some kind of medication?'

'Detective, clinical depression is a real, almost tangible thing. It can be horribly debilitating, even paralyzing, in a psychological sense. It can spring from many causes, like a chemical imbalance. I honestly think that was the nature of Jessica's problem. She needed treatment.'

'Were you considering hospitalizing her?'

'No. That would have been a last resort. But I honestly believed there was something physically wrong with her. I urged her to also visit her regular doctor, get a full physical. She would not do that either.' Orzibal stared intently first at Dan and then at Jilly. 'If she could have just been more open to the process. At heart she was a lovely woman, well-meaning, wanting to love her family and friends and to be loved by them. But she had hit a major roadblock, you might say. She was incapable of trusting or sharing with them. As she gradually withdrew from what support system she had left, it became a vicious circle: they grew impatient with her own behavior and withdrew from her. She felt terribly isolated. To be so alone, it's very painful on a deep level.'

'It must have been hard not only on her but on those around her,' Jilly observed.

'Undoubtedly.'

'Did you ever have the chance to talk to her friends, her husband, her children?'

'No. I suggested that perhaps it might do some good if her family members also began to see somebody. Not me, but someone else. She said absolutely not, they would never agree to that. Clearly she was the one against it.'

Jilly nodded. 'Did she ever talk about her husband, perhaps that she suspected him of infidelity?'

'We talked about that, yes. She increasingly believed that. I honestly don't know whether he was unfaithful, but what I stressed to her was to examine her feelings rationally and deal with them realistically. I tried to steer her out of restating a problem and into working out a solution. We got nowhere.'

'I understand he was devoting most of his time to work, his startup company.'

'What registered with her was that he spent the great majority of his time away from her. For someone who already felt marginalized and insulated, that was particularly difficult.'

'What about her children?'

'She often expressed frustration with their unwillingness to communicate with her or to show appreciation to her. The word she used most often was ungrateful.' She shrugged. 'They're teenagers. A most difficult phase of childhood under the best of circumstances.'

'Do you think she was being unrealistic in her assessments of her kids and her husband?'

'I honestly don't know. That was one of the things we were exploring. I'm afraid we weren't getting anywhere yet.'

'And the last time you saw her was about a year ago?'

'Yes, about fifteen months ago.'

Jilly sat back and shook her head. 'Doctor, I have to tell you, Jessica is a total mystery to us. We need something, anything, to help us reconstruct the hours and days prior to her death. In the time you saw her, was there ever anything she said or did that might give us some clue as to her actions of the past weekend? Any idea where she might have gone, who she might have seen, what she might have done?'

'My best guess,' the therapist replied slowly, looking back and forth at them both, 'is that she was likely by herself. In the time I saw her regularly, she was already steadily losing trust in everybody around her. She needed help, Detectives - if not from me, then somebody — and barring that, it would only get worse with time.'

★   ★   ★

'So we've got a troubled woman in isolation mode who doesn't seem to have been anywhere or talked to anyone after last Friday,' Jilly said, exhaling with exasperation. They were back in the car, pulling out of the parking lot beneath Orzibal's building.

'We've got so many things we need to cover,' said Dan. 'I feel bad I've made this more difficult and we can't split up.'

'Just keep your appointment, partner, and problem solved.'

'You know what the DMV is like. Even with an appointment, I might still have to wait.'

'At least you can still renew. If you'd put it off for 90 days, you would have had to start all over as if you needed a new license.'

'Yeah,' Dan said. 'There's that. I just feel so stupid.'

'You're not stupid, Dan. It just got by you.'

'Is this what it's like when you get older? Letting stuff get away?'

'You're asking me that because I'm so old?'

'Oh no, *no*. Sorry, Jilly. I'm really off my game today, aren't I?'

'Just keep the appointment tomorrow, will you? And listen, do me a favor — look up another number for us and let's make one more stop before we call it a day?'

'Sure. Who?'

'Natasha Hedgefield. The girlfriend.'

* * *

She wasn't surprised to have them show up at her front door. She took one look at their proffered IDs and simply said, 'James said you'd be coining. Come on in,' and opened the door to her small but airy condo.

Any expectations of James Pidgeon's 'other woman' as a femme fatale would have met with utter disappointment. Natasha Hedgefield was a straightforward, no-nonsense type. In an earlier time she would have been considered the 'girl next door,' of the nerdier variety, with straight shoulder-length brown hair, black-rimmed glasses, and a plain dark sweater and skirt. She seemed genuinely shocked by the death of Jessica Pidgeon and quite willing to speak with the detectives. Once more today, Jilly and Dan sat in still another parlor asking their questions. Natasha was not chatty; she spoke keenly and precisely, answering their questions directly.

'We understand you work for Mr.

Pidgeon, is that correct?' began Jilly.

'Yes, I'm head of software development for JRX. I've been with the company since its inception.'

Jilly watched her evenly. 'And you and Mr. Pidgeon are currently in a relationship? Outside of the workplace, that is?'

Natasha folded her arms and returned the even stare. 'Yes we are.'

'How long ago did it begin?'

'We started seeing each other socially maybe four or five months ago. He needed someone to talk to, first during work, then we'd have drinks or dinner. That sounds more romantic than it was. Mostly it was takeout at the office late nights while we worked. After a few weeks, we became closer. That was after he moved out of his house into an apartment here in the city.'

'So you two did not become intimately involved,' Dan said, 'until after he'd moved out of his house?'

Natasha nodded. 'It just sort of happened. He's been having a terrible time at home for a while now. Between that and the stresses of trying to get JRX off the ground, it's been tearing him up. Do you have any idea what it takes to establish a tech startup, even with a large dedicated team, which we do not have? We're talking seventy, eighty hours a week. And there was his intolerable family situation on top of that. I just happened to be the one person there for him. And, well ... things happened.'

'Can we talk about his 'family situation'?' Jilly asked.

'I didn't want to come between him and his wife,' Natasha said firmly, still staring at Jilly. 'For a long time he seemed to genuinely care about her. He was trying to find some way to make things work. It wasn't until I was convinced that was over that I allowed myself to ... well, to become involved with James.'

Magnanimous of you, Jilly thought but didn't say. 'What exactly was happening?'

'She was just getting stranger and stranger. Began accusing him of all sorts of things. And then there were the kids. They were constantly fighting with him.'

'They're teenagers,' Jilly said. 'It's not unusual for them to be difficult.'

'Yes, well, I don't know about that. I know nothing about kids. I just know James found them frustrating. Nobody was getting along in that house. The kids, the wife, James, they were all at odds with one another. What a zoo. He'd leave one pressure cooker and go to another.'

'We understand she was being treated, possibly for depression.'

Natasha pursed her lips. 'It didn't sound to me like she was being *treated*. She was just a neurotic, unhappy witch.'

'You said she was making accusations,' interjected Dan. 'What kind of accusations?'

'Everything and anything. She didn't think he was bringing home enough money so she decided he must be spending it somewhere else. It was a startup! The money takes time. She never understood that. All she remembered was his salary from when he worked for a big tech company. She always complained about the bills and the expenses, but they had a nice house, nice cars, good schools for the kids. He was paying the bills and keeping everything going. I don't know, maybe she was accustomed to spending a lot on herself and no longer had it. Then she complained he wasn't home enough, that he wasn't spending time with her or the kids. And then she got it in her head that the reason for all that was that James was seeing another woman. Maybe several women. I think it grew into an elaborate fantasy. She had no idea what it took to create a new company, to make it a success. There was no money and there was no time.'

Dan and Jilly silently exchanged knowing looks. 'Did you ever meet her?' Jilly asked.

'Once or twice, casually. We never really talked much. Anyway, my point is, she drove him out. Her and those kids.'

'And,' Jilly said pointedly, 'as the cliché goes, right into your arms?'

Natasha's eyes blazed angrily. 'Look, I'm trying to help you here. Whatever happened to her was terrible and I'm sorry for her. But James had nothing to do with this. He cared for her. He tried his best, and in the end he had to get out. When they sold the company to Ubertech, he would have made a lot of money and could have divorced her and taken care of her. He had no reason to do anything to get rid of her because he was already gone. The reason he wound up with me was, yes, because she pushed him away. She was sick.'

'Yes,' sighed Jilly. 'She was.' She was a woman who needed help desperately. And there was none to be had.

*　★　*

'You've been quiet,' Jilly said to Dan as they drove back to the station.

'We've seen lots worse. Why does this one bother me so much?'

'I know what you mean. Quite a lineup of winners in Jessica's life, wasn't there?'

'The husband's a piece of work,' mused Dan. 'But I just don't see him as the killer.'

'Me neither. His girlfriend made a good point. He'd escaped. With the upcoming buyout he could have paid Jessica off and been free. It made no sense to kill her.'

'And especially not in that way. That was a brutal crime of passion, and he's pretty passive.'

'There was a lot of hate in that,' Jilly agreed. 'Maybe there's a side to him we haven't seen past that passive aggression.'

'I'm going by what you've taught me, Jilly, to trust my gut. We can't stop considering him but we need to cast a wider net.'

'I taught you that? I guess I'm pretty good after all.'

'Never for a moment ever doubted that,' Dan said, forcing a small smile despite himself.

6

Sometimes luck just happens. It might be good or bad, or it might turn out to be totally different from what it at first seems ...

The two teenagers skulking on the side street in the dark couldn't have felt too lucky. It was a slow night on one of their usual swings around the neighborhood. Generally, four in the morning in the middle of the week was prime time for enterprising thievery. Most residents had long since gone to bed and wouldn't be waking up to get ready for work for some time yet. Auto alarms had for the most part been abandoned here, since they were seen as nothing more than annoyances; nobody ever actually responded to them. It was remarkable how many car doors were left unlocked and windows partly opened. Quick silent swoops usually yielded easy swag to be resold, but tonight there were no open doors or windows.

Refusing to go home empty-handed, they had begun carefully peeking into dark houses and garages and had found a crack in a painted-over alley window on a dilapidated old stucco garage set back off the street, far from the closest street light. It had been easy to push the glass in to make a large enough space for one of them to crawl through. The shards of glass fell almost silently inside, apparently falling onto piles of cloth or newspaper.

'You go in, Littleboy,' muttered the taller one, looking furtively back to the street. 'You fit better.'

The smaller kid squeezed through the pane into the shadows of the garage. 'Dark in here,' he whispered. 'Can't see nothin'.'

The tall teen pulled a cheap plastic butane lighter out of the pocket of his hoodie and passed it through the windowpane. 'Here. See if there's anything you can just hand out.' He cast another nervous look out at the street. 'Hurry!'

'Give me a second ...' came the voice from inside the darkened space. There were several flicking sounds of the flint. Then there was a spark of light.

And then there was a sudden brighter flash.

'Oh damn!' shouted the kid from inside, and instantly his head stuck through the windowpane, a panicked expression on his face. Flames flickered behind him. He frantically tried to jam himself back through the window. All of a sudden it felt a quarter of the size it had been when he entered. The bigger guy was already in motion, running back to the street. 'Hey! Don't leave me here, Freddie! Help me!'

He struggled to break through the window, cracking more glass panes and splintering wooden strips in the process. It took him a long time, his own panic making it all the harder to extract himself. In his mind a horrific inferno had erupted in the garage, although in reality only a small pile of old newspapers had caught fire. He finally popped himself free, landing on the ground outside the garage. He was bolting down the alley just as the first fire engine had turned down the street, sirens blazing. Somebody must have turned in the alarm almost immediately.

Damn the luck, he thought. Sometimes

you'd wait forever for cops or firemen. This would be the time that they'd be right on the scene. How did they get there so *fast*? Everything was just bad luck tonight. He ran as fast as he could, panting and gasping.

Firemen were soon breaking open the garage's shoddy door and were able to extinguish the fire before it could have spread and engulfed the old building. Uniformed police were already arriving on the scene.

One of the unis stopped to talk to one of the firemen in front of the still-smoldering garage. 'That's a weird one.'

'Yeah. Must have been somebody trying to break in through that window. They touched off a stack of newspapers and magazines right underneath it. Good thing we just happened to be a couple blocks away.'

The police officer pointed at the car sitting inside the garage, scorched but reasonably unscathed by the fire. 'That's a pretty nice car for this kind of garage, don't you think?'

'I'll tell you,' said the fireman, 'if I owned a late model Audi like that, I sure as hell wouldn't be keeping it in a garbage can like this.'

The officer nodded, pressing a button on a shoulder microphone as he noted the plate number. 'There's only one reason I can think of for someone to put a car like that in a building like this.'

* * *

Dan and Jilly both hung up their phones almost simultaneously and looked at one another across the aisle between their desks. Thursday morning was already in full gear.

'You first,' said Dan.

'There are no available techs to check Jessica's room and computer for at least another twenty-four hours. But I finally spoke with Wilhelm Gauss of Ubertech in Portland and with the airline. It would seem that James Pidgeon is covered for Sunday and he was on the flight returning here Monday morning.' She looked expectantly at Dan.

'The only good news I've got is that you won't have to do all the driving after I renew my license this afternoon. Everything else was a bust. I was on the phone with several people from Laurie's school before I could finally get hold of a guidance counselor who would even talk to me.'

'And?'

'Pure stonewall. She said we'd need the permission of the parents to talk with any of Laurie's friends. Wouldn't give me any contact info. The best I could do was to get her to contact the boyfriend's parents and have them contact us.'

'Roberto you mean?'

'Yep. I'm thinking we're going to have to go down there and be a little more insistent.'

Jilly folded her arms in frustration and leaned back, biting her lip. 'Any minute now, Castillo's going to be coming out of his office reminding us about the pressure coming down. We have to find something.'

'We've still got Marmaduke.'

'And he's not good for this until we can establish motive and opportunity. We can't even place Jessica anywhere up until the moment her body was placed in that receptacle. If we can't put them together in a believable manner, any half-decent lawyer is going to have an easy time walking him.'

It was a technique that Dan had learned

from Jilly: go over everything still one more time and hope to see something new. He idly played with his pen as he narrated the scenario again. 'Jessica Pidgeon never leaves her house. She's experiencing severe depression and maybe some paranoia. Maybe she's close to a breakdown. All of a sudden late on a Sunday night, she has a burst of activity. She leaves the house, somewhere she writes a strange letter on someone else's computer, admits to drug use that nobody else finds believable, signs it in a strange way, drives to an unfamiliar ATM out of her comfort zone, withdraws the maximum amount, puts the money and letter in an envelope that she's already prepared and addressed to Melinda, and drops it into a strange post office box.'

'You're thinking what we considered earlier, that she was being coerced?' said Jilly. 'That she was hoping to subtly tell us something?'

'It's all that makes sense to me at this point.'

'I don't see Marmaduke being a part of that.'

'No. Maybe the letter and the robbery

and murder are two separate incidents. Maybe someone convinced her to send the money and left, she went off to do it, and then Marmaduke caught up with her.'

'Or maybe Marmaduke has nothing to do with it. Maybe he really did just happen upon her wallet after she was killed.'

Dan nodded thoughtfully, still staring at his pen. 'We have to keep him in the picture because of the physical evidence, but yeah, I somehow don't think he's our guy.'

'A lot of maybes,' Jilly said. 'We need a for-sure of some kind.'

Dan's phone began to ring. 'Hold on a minute, Jilly.' He picked up the receiver. 'Detective Lee.'

'It's Sandy Kovetsky, Dan. Do you believe in pure dumb luck?'

'Officer Kovetsky. I'm not sure. Why?'

'I'm about to show you proof it exists. We found your victim's Audi last night.'

'What? Are you sure?'

'Gray A4, two years old. I ran the plate this morning. Registered to Jessica Pidgeon in Farmington.'

'Where? Where was it?' Dan had grabbed a pad and was energetically jotting notes.

Jilly, noting his excitement, rose from her desk and joined him.

'Locked up in a moldy old garage on Warwick Street, a few blocks from Sheffield. Looks like some kids broke into it and set it on fire. My partner and I were nearby and arrived just after the fire engines. They put out the fire pretty quickly. It didn't have a chance to spread too far. The car got a little singed but it's otherwise okay. The arson investigators are there and SID is on its way now.'

'Did you look the car over?'

'Just perfunctory. There's all kinds of stuff scattered around on the front seat and floor. Some jewelry. What looks like some sort of narcotics, I'd say oxy.'

'Whose garage is it?'

'We're not sure yet. There's an adjoining house but it seems deserted. Nobody answered the door and it looks like nobody's been in there for a long time.'

'We'll be right over.'

'Sadly, I won't be there. It's been some night. I'm heading home. Good luck.'

'What's the address?' Dan noted it down, said a few more words, then told her they were on the way over. Jilly was already hanging over his desk, eager to hear what was happening. Dan told her.

Castillo was just stepping out of his office as they rushed by, almost colliding with him.

'I was about to ask you for an update,' the Lieutenant said.

'We got a break, Lou,' said Dan, not bothering to stop or even slow down. 'They found her car. We're heading there now.'

'Fill me in when you get back!' Castillo yelled after them as they headed for the stairwell. He wasn't sure whether they heard him or not.

★   ★   ★

The uniforms on the scene confirmed that the house next to the garage was unoccupied. Somehow the SID and arson investigation teams had managed to maintain a complicated dance around one another and stay out of each other's way. Counting Dan and Jilly, there were now nine people in the small garage, but they had avoided the potential for chaos and were working in surprising harmony. There seemed a clear demarcation of territories arrived at either tacitly or explicitly; the arson people stayed to their side of the garage while the SID people concentrated on the scorched car and the remainder of the garage.

The head of the SID team was a man named Smithers, whose youthful appearance belied his experience. The detectives knew him well. He had greeted them upon their arrival and apprised them of the situation. He pointed to the Audi, which was filling up much of the small garage.

'The car was unlocked, front windows down. The garage door was locked; whoever put the car in here must have had a key. There were no signs of anything being forced.' He pointed to the front seat of the car, where a jump-suited tech was snapping photos. 'We're almost done and then you can have it. Nothing in the trunk but the jack and the spare in the well. We found a baseball glove in the back seat, but otherwise nothing back there. There are blood stains on the rear seats. Possible signs of a struggle or violence. There was quite a bit of material in the front, scattered around the floor mat on the passenger side. We'll bag it and take it as soon as you've had a chance to look it all over.'

'Thanks,' said Jilly, she and Dan already pulling on new pairs of gloves.

Dan picked up items one by one, carefully looked them over and handed them back to Jilly, who handled them just as gingerly. A plain gold necklace with a simple oval pendant holding a single blue stone. A simple gold ring set with three tiny blue stones. Two long golden earrings in a broad teardrop shape. The wire hooks at the ends of them were blotched with brownish stains.

'We found what appears to be flesh residue in the earrings,' Smithers said, watching them. 'We took the samples. We'll also run the dried blood on the hooks.'

Jilly nodded. *Jessica's earrings, apparently ripped from her pierced ears ...*

Dan held up an orange plastic prescription container. He shook it gently. He opened the top and looked inside. 'Oxycodone is my guess. Six tablets. No label.' He handed it to Jilly. She peered at the pastel-colored tablets.

Jessica didn't use any drugs. She hated

medication in general ...

A cheap plastic felt-tip pen. Dan pulled off the cap. Either black or dark blue.

Blue ink stains on Jessica's fingers. Her name signed on the letter in dark blue ink.

The baseball glove in the back seat was a fairly new, expensive fielder's model that smelled of oiled leather. BRAD PIDGEON had been neatly inscribed in capitals with marker along the back of one of the fingers. As the tech had said, there was nothing else in the rear.

Jilly's eyes wandered across the garage. Under normal circumstances it would have been a dark place — there were only two painted-over windows, now broken, along the alley side — but the investigators had set up lighting stanchions in the corners. The space was now extremely bright, and details stood out to her. There was a small cluttered workbench in the back corner covered with tools, car parts and crushed empty beer cans. Similar items littered the ground nearby: cans of oil, more tools, screws and nails, cardboard boxes of different sizes. More beer bottles and cans. Scattered piles of magazines and papers. A small old refrigerator sat underneath the workbench. The entire garage looked as if it hadn't been occupied or used in some time. There were webs and a coat of dust everywhere.

Not quite everywhere.

Jilly walked to the corner and reached down for the one gleaming item, apparently jammed into the corner debris, that did not seem to be covered in dust or grime. She carefully lifted it up with thumb and forefinger.

'What do you make of this?' she called out. Dan and Smithers both turned to look at her.

A bright silver aluminum baseball bat. The kind that high school and middle school teams might use.

Gingerly holding the knob at the end of the handle, she rotated it, making it glint in the bright lights. The darker spots near the top of the barrel were perfectly clear.

'I think we've found our murder weapon,' she said.

★   ★   ★

Dan punched off the connection on his cellphone as they headed back to the station. 'The entire block is rental property, all apparently owned by an out-of-state company and maintained by a local property management agency. I got voice mail at the management.' The impatience was evident in his voice. 'We can probably do this just as fast online when we get back.'

'We're still a huge step up. She was murdered either in or near her car before she was dumped. And the pen ... it wasn't a random robbery. Someone made her sign those letters, and that means they also made her take out the money. This directly involves Melinda.'

'Clearly ... but some things don't add up if that's true. She doesn't seem capable of that kind of murder. Just on the basis of not being strong enough or vicious enough.'

'But she was desperate,' Jilly pointed out. 'She could have gotten someone else to do it for her.'

'Or,' suggested Dan, 'someone took it upon themselves to act on her behalf. Or what they saw as being on her behalf.'

'The stuff in the car. Her jewelry. The narcotics. By everybody's account she didn't use any kind of drugs. Her wallet was taken but not her jewelry. Why were those in the car?'

'Hopefully we can get the fingerprinting on those things expedited.'

* * *

Dan seemed to be having a somewhat frustrating telephone conversation with the management firm. Jilly saw him fidgeting at his desk and jotting notes as he spoke. Her own desk phone rang.

'This is Mallory at the front desk. There's a kid here to see you, one of your victim's kids.'

Laurie? 'Send her up.'

'It's not a her. He's on his way.'

She hung up and shouted, 'Dan!'

Jilly was waiting when the elevator doors opened.

'You must be Brad, right?'

He was short and looked younger than his age, wearing a hooded sweatshirt, an unruly mop of brown hair, and a nervous expression. He shrugged. 'You must be the detective.'

'I'm Jilly Garvey. Come on in.' She led him down a hall to an interview room, sterile and uninviting but quieter than the bustling squad room. Dan was already seated, waiting.

'Have a seat. This is my partner, Dan Lee. Do you want something, a Coke maybe?'

The boy shook his head, looking apprehensively around the room.

'Hi, Brad,' said Dan, trying to manage a smile. 'Is it okay if we call you Brad? Do you have a nickname, or ...?'

'No, that's fine.'

'How did you get here?' Dan asked him. 'Shouldn't you be at school?'

'School's not important right now. The bus from Farmington is easy. One transfer and I'm a block away from here.'

'The bus goes through some kind of sketchy areas. Even in the daytime, isn't it kind of scary?'

'I can take care of myself.'

Jilly smiled to herself. Young teens. They were oblivious to the world around them.

There was a rock song with the line 'immortal for a limited time.' After what had happened to his mother, she would have thought he'd be terrified to go out into the dangerous world.

'Why did you come here, Brad?' Dan asked. 'Why didn't you just call us?'

Brad shrugged. 'I found your card in my sister's room. I didn't want to go to school today so I decided to come here instead.'

'Why?'

The boy stared down at his hands on the table for a long time. 'It's not right. It's just not right.'

'You mean, what happened to your mom? No. It's not.'

'Not just that,' he muttered quietly. 'Nobody cares what happened.'

'We care,' said Dan.

'I mean, *they* don't. It's like nothing ever happened. They won't talk about it. They pretend like everything is okay.' He looked up at Jilly. He looked as if he was trying not to cry. 'Nothing's okay. Nothing.'

'Brad, are you willing to talk about it? Is there anything you can tell us that might help us?' said Jilly.

177

'My mom got really strange lately. Something was wrong. She was scared.'

'Scared of what?'

'It's not like there was something to be scared of. She started making things up. She thought we were turning against her. She wouldn't talk *to* us. All she would do was yell at us, then she'd go somewhere to be alone and not talk at all, for hours sometimes.'

'I think your mother might have been … well, she might have been sick,' Jilly said.

Brad nodded, looking down at the table again. He spoke quietly. They had to lean in to listen. 'Two kids in my school killed themselves in the last year. The teachers said they were depressed.'

'That's awful. I'm sorry. Did you know them well?'

'One of them, yeah. She was a friend of mine. The other one, not really. They both kept to themselves a lot, didn't talk to people.'

Jilly saw the connection, why Brad was bringing this up.

'They spent a lot of time talking to us in the classroom and the general assemblies afterward. They said things like, we should ask for help if we're unhappy. That we should look for signs in our friends, tell someone.'

'Good advice,' said Dan.

'But the problem is, if someone's depressed, it's not like they want to ask for help, you know? It seems like they just want to somehow make themselves a real pain in the butt, to drive their friends further away. I don't think many people would have wanted to help the kids in my school, even if they knew. Not too many kids liked them.'

Jilly thought to herself, *My God, this kid has more insight than most adults I know.*

'I think that's what happened with my mom. She drove everybody away. She didn't see anybody as ... someone who could help, you know? Everybody was just ... someone trying to make it harder for her.'

'So none of you were getting along with her. She was isolating.' Jilly was getting tired of that word.

Brad nodded and wiped an eye.

'What happened with Melinda and your mom, Brad? Were you there when they argued?'

He nodded again. 'It was after school. My mom was out and Melinda had driven us home. Laurie's friend Robbie came back with her. They had a project they were working on together.'

'Robbie is Laurie's boyfriend, right?'

'No, not exactly. They're just good friends. I mean, I don't think they're like boyfriend and girlfriend. Laurie doesn't really have any regular boyfriends. But my mom thought he was.'

'I understand she didn't approve of Robbie hanging out with Laurie.'

'No, she hated him. I don't know why. He's a really nice guy. He's really smart in certain ways, like he knows how stuff works and how things are put together, you know? He has trouble in school. He wants to be a mechanic like his dad. But he's got to pass his academics and he doesn't do real well in them. He wanted to quit school and go work in a garage. Laurie was trying to get him to finish school. She was tutoring him. Secretly.'

'Why secretly?'

'Because he was ashamed, and because my mom didn't want her to see him. They had a math test coming up and it was really important and Robbie was worried he wasn't going to pass it, so he had come home with her so she could help him study. Laurie's really good at math. She helps me all the time. But she had to sneak him in while my mom wasn't home.'

'And Melinda knew.'

'Yeah. She liked Robbie and was trying to get him to finish school too. She felt school was really important. She understood what was really going on. So when Laurie asked if Robbie could get a lift home with us, Melinda said sure, even though she knew how Mom felt. She wanted to do the right thing.'

'Let me guess. Your mother came home unexpectedly?'

Robbie nodded again, head still down. 'She was in a terrible mood. I'd seen her bad but this was the worst. They — I mean Laurie and Robbie — were in Laurie's room. She, I mean my mom, went nuts. Started screaming and raving. It was the worst fit she ever threw. She started saying all sorts of totally crazy stuff about what Laurie and Robbie were doing behind her back. She accused them of skipping school and coming back to spend the day in Laurie's room. She yelled at Robbie and chased him out of the house. Then she turned on Melinda. She called her a conspirator, helping Laurie sneak around behind her back. She worked out this whole crazy plot in her head as she went along, that maybe they hadn't even gone to school that day and Melinda had driven them right back to our house after my mom had gone out. It was nuts. Melinda was trying to talk sense to her, but my mom just told her she was fired, to get out right then. She took out a bunch of money and shoved it at her.'

'Where were you while all this was happening?'

'I was in the living room, texting on my phone, just trying to be somewhere else. I felt awful and stayed quiet. I hunkered down into the cushions. I don't know if she even noticed I was there.'

'And Laurie?'

'Laurie went crazy, called my mom a delusional maniac, and ran up to her room. She was crying and hollering.'

'So your mother ordered Melinda out of

the house, told her not to come back?'

'Uh-huh. She tried to reason with my mom but it was impossible. She got really angry herself, picked up her things and walked out. She drove home and never came back.'

'Did you like Melinda?'

Now several tears rolled along Brad's nose and cheeks. He stammered slightly. 'She was the last sane one in the house. She was our last friend. Especially for Laurie.'

'What about your dad?'

Brad shook his head sharply. 'She drove him away a long time ago. He hasn't been there for us in a long time.'

The detectives sat in silence for some time.

'What was your mother like after that, Brad?' Dan finally asked.

'It's like she wasn't there. She was like a zombie in one of those movies, the walking dead. She almost never went out; she hardly ever spoke to us. We pretty much got ourselves up and ready for school. She'd drive us to school, or me to baseball practice, or Laurie to study groups, but she wouldn't say a word. She was like a robot behind the wheel. I don't know if Laurie and my mom ever spoke again.'

'And then you went to your grand-mother's a few days later.' Brad nodded.

And never saw your mother again, Jilly thought to herself.

7

'You don't need to drive me to the DMV,' Dan continued to protest as they crossed the parking lot to the car. 'It's not that far. The bus is easy enough.'

'Just like Brad said, huh? The bus is easy. This is easier. Come on, get in.' Jilly hit the remote and the *click* of the car door locks resounded. As they opened the doors, she paused.

'What?' asked Dan, looking across the top of the car at her.

'The bus is easy,' she repeated.

'Yeah. And …?'

'Jessica didn't drive to somewhere in the city and get stopped by anybody. Somebody came to her house and made her drive them away.'

Dan nodded, digesting that for a few moments. 'Okay. Yeah.'

'She was saying and doing a lot of regrettable things. There were a lot of people who weren't very happy with her.'

'The husband. The daughter. The boy-friend. The housekeeper. And so on.'

'The husband was gone, and so were the kids. I don't think it was the boyfriend, or whatever you want to call him.'

'Where are you taking this?'

'The pen in the car. Someone had brought those letters, already prepared, and forced Jessica to sign them; to withdraw the money — that was the maximum she could get from her ATM at one time — to be sent to Melinda.'

'So back to Melinda?'

Jilly bit her lip, following her train of thought. 'Not Melinda. She's not right for it. Plus … she's got a car. She would have driven over. I think whoever took Jessica came by the bus. I know this is all a jump but I have a feeling.'

'And your gut is telling you not Melinda.'

'No. Someone who knows Melinda. Someone who cared a *lot* about her getting fired.'

'If she's out of work, the daughter doesn't get to go to college,' Dan said, picking up the chain of thought. 'Or thinks she doesn't. But we saw the daughter. Olivia, right?

She's kind of an aesthetic figure. I can't see her committing that kind of violence.'

'No. But she could have friends. She must have friends.'

They got into the car and closed the doors. As Jilly started up the engine she said, 'I need to go have another talk with Melinda while you get your paperwork done.'

★   ★   ★

Dan only had to stand in the DEPARTMENT OF MOTOR VEHICLES — VISITORS WITH APPOINTMENTS line for seven minutes, which he figured was doing relatively well. An extremely bored elderly woman gazed blankly at him through smeared bifocals.

'I have an appointment to renew my license,' Dan said, holding up his printed form.

'Well, aren't you special, honey,' she said in a voice that would cut crystal. She took the form from him, scribbled something upon it, stamped it, and handed it back to him. 'Window 16.' He looked in the direction she was pointing and saw another line of six or seven people. She was already rasping out '*Next!*' so he shrugged and moved on.

As he stepped to the back of the line at Window 16, his cell phone rang. He checked the readout: it showed an out-of-town area code, 832.

'This is Detective Lee.'

'You're the detective, right?' The voice was unfamiliar: deep, thick-tongued. Perhaps the guy had been drinking a bit.

'This is Detective Lee. Who's this?'

'My name is Tyrone Watney. The rental guy said you wanted to talk with me.'

The caller now had all of Dan's attention. For a moment, the line and the DMV did not exist. 'You're the lessee of the house and garage on Warwick Street?'

'Lessee means I rent it? Then yeah, I am. I haven't been there in about four months though.'

'What do you mean?'

'I been in the Houston area. Started out as a road trip, you know? Then I had an accident and my car broke down and I was in the hospital for a while … well, story short, I just decided to stay here until my luck changed.'

'Hold on. You haven't been here in town in four months?'

'Uh-uh. One thing just led to another. I got a temporary job here, bartending. I owe a few people some money here and, well, they aren't gonna let me leave until I pay them, you know?'

Fascinating life saga, reflected Dan, *but please spare me.* 'But you still rent the house and the garage on Warwick?'

'Well, yeah.' He said it as if it were the most obvious thing in the world. 'I just send them a money order every month. I got a lease.'

Dan ran a hand across his forehead. 'Mr. Watney ... is there anybody else who might have access to your home or your garage?'

'As a matter of fact,' Tyrone said, 'yeah. Got friends who like to work on their cars, change their oil and like that. Maybe drink a few beers and hang out. The police there aren't too friendly with them working on their cars in the street, and they sure don't like 'em drinking in public. They get kinda touchy like that. No offense.'

Dan sighed. 'None taken. Anybody in particular?'

'Well,' said Tyrone hesitantly, 'there's one guy I lent the keys to before I left. I got a lot of newspapers and stuff in there and he said he'd clean them out for me. Helpful kinda guy. What's this about, anyway? The agent wouldn't tell me nothin'. Am I in any trouble here or something?' Tyrone sounded as if he dreaded anymore trouble.

'No, sir, if you're telling me the truth about being out of town for the past few months.'

'Gospel truth, Detective! I got plenty of people who can vouch for me!'

'Then, no, I can't say that you're in any trouble here, as long as you can tell me the name of this helpful guy you lent your keys to.'

Tyrone sounded most happy to do just that.

★   ★   ★

As Jilly approached Melinda's building, she saw the same bespectacled young man sitting on the stoop that she had encountered before, again reading a paperback book. He looked up as she reached the steps.

'You're back,' he said, looking her in the eye seriously.

'You're Terry, am I right?'

He grinned, a huge bright smile that seemed to change his whole demeanor. 'Well now, how is it you know that?'

'I'm a detective, Terry, remember? Actually, Melinda told me.'

His smile faded but did not disappear. He looked amused. 'I'm not sure she's here right now, Detective.'

'I'm going to check for myself.' Jilly continued to mount the stairs. As she passed him, he looked up at her and said, 'Do you honestly think she killed that lady?'

'I don't think anything, Terry. I'm just trying to learn the facts.'

'I've known Melinda Barstow for a number of years now. We've been close friends. She is an excellent mother and a wonderful lady. There's nobody with more integrity in this entire city. Why can't you leave her alone?'

Jilly paused at the door to the apartment building. 'If she's innocent, she'll help me solve this. She's got nothing to fear. I suggest you stay out of it, unless you've got something to help me?'

Terry shrugged and turned back to his book. Over his shoulder he muttered, 'Not a thing. Except I guarantee Melinda hasn't done anything. She's good people.'

Melinda's apartment was one flight up from the interior lobby and about halfway down the corridor. Jilly noticed that Melinda's door was slightly ajar as she approached. She stopped and knocked on the door and called out, 'Melinda? Ms. Barstow?'

The strains of a classical serenade came from her bag. Her phone ring tone. 'Yeah, hello.'

'Jilly, it's Dan.'

'Don't tell me you're done already! I'll be over for you in a —'

'No, Jilly, listen. I just got a call from the guy who leases the house and the garage.'

'Yeah?'

'He's in Houston or thereabouts. He claims he hasn't been here in several months. He lets his friends use the garage to work on their cars and hang out.'

'Great. That's not much help.'

Nobody had yet answered the door. Jilly, caught up in the conversation, was momentarily distracted from what little ambient noise there was in the quiet hall. She didn't hear the hushed footsteps coming quickly.

'He says there's one guy who borrowed his keys just before he left town and still has them.'

'Okay, does this guy have a name?'

'Yeah. Terry Blaze. He says he's Caribbean of some variety. He lives over near Melinda's street. Wasn't that guy we ran into out front named Terry?'

'Oh damn,' said Jilly. Ignoring her phone, she instinctively reached into her bag for her automatic. All at once she felt the hand on the back of her neck and felt herself being driven forcefully against Melinda's front door.

8

She never lost consciousness but things got a little confused for a short time. She remembered pitching forward into the apartment and falling onto the floor. She rolled around and began to sit up. She saw her bag and phone several feet away on the floor, and started to go for the bag. A husky arm reached down and pushed her back to the floor.

'Don't move,' said Terry, towering over her. Suddenly he looked much bigger than he had seemed before. His hulking figure obscured the doorway as he reached back and slammed the door behind him.

Her bag was on the floor, scant feet away, but she didn't turn her gaze to it. If she could just reach her gun ...

'Where's Melinda?' she asked, glaring up at him.

'I honestly don't know. She's not here, though.'

'Did you hurt her?'

'*No!*' Terry almost screamed, his eyes widening in disbelief. 'Hurt her? Never! I could never hurt her! You really don't get it, do you?'

Jilly slowly brought herself to a sitting position, staring up at the man who now seemed to be a giant, staring down at her menacingly. The glasses didn't make him look academic anymore. Somehow they made him more ominous.

'I told you not to move!' he bellowed, his eyes widening. 'Why can't you women ever do what you're told!' He started to reach down to push her back, but stopped when Jilly flinched slightly, involuntarily. She silently cursed herself for it but at least he didn't knock her down again.

'She didn't do what you told her, did she?' Jilly said quietly, locking eyes with the man looming over her. How could she have not noticed how big he was? Did he just suddenly become this frightening giant? She pushed back the fear and forced herself to think calmly.

'She? What are you talking about?'

'You know who I mean,' she continued, slowly continuing to raise herself up. No sudden moves. Slow but steady. Keep talking. Keep him involved. 'Jessica Pidgeon. She wouldn't do what you wanted, would she?'

'Damn her,' Terry growled.

'She got you angry, didn't she? Is that why you killed her?'

She hit the nerve.

'She had no right!' Terry exclaimed. 'Ruining people's lives, lying and stealing!'

'What did she steal, Terry?' Slowly moving around. She forced herself not to look directly toward her bag as she calculated the distance and the direct line to it.

'She stole their lives!' he yelled. He was getting angrier by the moment. He had a deep voice but an emotional whine was creeping into it. 'Melinda worked for that woman for *years*! She took care of them! She did their scut work — things they weren't willing to do themselves! Smug, selfish rich people, never want to get their hands dirty! Those kids — Melinda was more a parent to them than either of those two ever were! And then that crazy witch accuses her of that stupid nonsense, fires her, after all those years won't even give her a *reference* …'

If she wasn't able to reach the bag, she would have to try to defend herself against him. That wasn't the optimum solution. He had a lot of size and weight on her. All she would have going for her was her police training, though that was hardly negligible. She had kept up her self-defense skills. She wouldn't be a scared, slight little woman unable to fight back. At least he didn't have a weapon, as far as she could tell. No baseball bat this time.

'Melinda can't get another job. Nobody's gonna hire her! They'll have to move away from here, from all of us! Olivia won't get to go to college! That girl is so damned intelligent! She's got a *life* ahead of her, better than her mom or me! It's not right to have that taken away from her!'

'So she got you angry, right?' Jilly continued, keeping her voice calm. 'You didn't set out to kill her, did you, Terry? You just set out to make things right again. You went to her house to convince her to make it up to Melinda.'

Terry just glowered at her, his jaw set. A teary gleam appeared in both of his eyes.

'You went to her house, didn't you? Maybe took a bus? You figured you'd talk to her? You were trying to be a good friend, Terry, you were trying to help them. You're a good friend, right?'

'I am a good friend! I'm the best friend they got!'

'So you took the bus there, did you?'

'Of course, how else was I gonna get there! Got no car!'

'But she wouldn't listen to you, is that what happened? You argued? Things got out of hand?'

'Stuck-up witch!' he hissed, and smacked one of his fists into the palm of his other hand. For a moment Jilly thought he was going to turn on her. The seething transformation of his blind anger was amazing, morphing him into something different, something less rational. 'Called Melinda some terrible names. Called *me* some terrible names.'

'So what did you do, Terry?'

'I was just gonna have her sign the letter, give me some money to put in with it. Tell Melinda she had a drug problem, that was why she acted the way she did. I was gonna scare her, tell her if she ever told anybody I was there, I'd come back and hurt her. But she didn't get scared. She said she'd tell everybody the minute I left. She'd call the police.'

Jilly couldn't see that as Terry's actual plan. He couldn't leave her there. There was the oxycodone. Maybe he was going to drug her, maybe even forcibly overdose her. But Jilly needed him to consider that she was buying his story.

'Okay. So you couldn't just leave her there. She wasn't cooperating. She disrespected you. That got you angry. So you decided to, what, have her drive you both somewhere?'

He shook his head, putting the fingers of one hand to his temple, lips moving silently. For a moment he seemed to be trying to tell himself the story. 'I don't remember too many details. She got me madder and madder. I remember I pushed her into her car and told her to drive into the city. It was a Sunday, no banks open but plenty of ATMs. I remember making her tell me the name of her bank and looking for a machine as we drove.'

'As you drove … where, Terry? Where did you want her to take you?' She put her weight on one knee and began to raise herself up more.

'I told you to sit *still*!' he suddenly roared. Too quick a move that time. Jilly held up her hands in placation.

'Okay, okay. Just getting more comfortable, okay? It's a hard floor down here! I want to hear your story. You want me to hear your story, don't you? Help me understand. So your plan was to have her sign a letter you wrote that made her sound like she had a drug problem, and put in some money for Melinda. Then you were going to, what, take her somewhere? Lock her up maybe?'

'I wasn't gonna hurt her!' he wailed. 'Yeah, maybe lock her up, I had a place I could keep her for a while. I don't know! I thought I'd planned it all really intelligently. But in the end I didn't really think it out all that carefully. I just knew I had to help Melinda and Olivia!'

'I can see that, Terry. You were trying to be a good friend. Things got out of hand.'

'Damn straight they did! *Way* out of hand.'

'You had drugs with you. You had oxy.'

'Yeah. Got it from a friend. Easy to find down here.'

'You wanted her to take the oxy, right? Maybe she'd pass out and you'd leave her to be found by someone, they'd assume she was muddled and had a problem, something like that?'

Terry shook his head and wrung his hands in the air in frustration. 'I don't know, something like that!'

'You were just trying to make it right,' Jilly repeated. The words seemed to have a little effect on him, bringing him down just a bit when she said them. 'And everything went wrong.'

He shook his head, tears trickling down his cheeks. All of a sudden he smacked his fist into his palm again, hard. The *smack* resonated in the small quiet apartment.

Outside somewhere, far away, Jilly swore she could hear a siren. She remembered she hadn't broken off the phone connection with Dan before Terry attacked her. It gave her hope. She prayed Terry didn't detect the siren as well.

Keep him talking.

'You must have gotten awfully angry, Terry. You hurt her terribly. I can't believe you wanted to do that. You're a good guy, right? You look out for women and kids, people smaller and not as strong as you.'

'Yes!' he hoarsely whispered, bending lower and looking at her searchingly. 'Yes! I am a good man! I care about the folks in the neighborhood! I *help* people! I don't hurt them! But sometimes people can just get me going ...'

'She pushed you to your limit, right? Something went too far. What happened?'

'I don't know! I don't remember! I just ... went nuts!'

'Where were you? Do you remember how it started?'

'I told her to take out a lot of money from her ATM. I was careful to stay out of any possible camera. She told me the most she could take out was four hundred. So I told her to take that. Then I had her drive us a little further, to a bad neighborhood, quiet. No people around at night. I had the letter all set up already. Made her sign it right there, in the car. Told her to take the oxy. She said no, she'd never take it. She didn't seem too scared. Looked me right in the eye, with that arrogant look. It was like she wanted to tick me off. That got me even madder.'

'And then what happened?'

'I don't know. I dragged her out of the car, I remember that. Told her she needed to listen to me, do what I said. I started hitting her in a side alley. Kept telling her to do what I said. I was yelling and yelling at her and she wasn't answering and I kept saying *answer me*. Then she was just lying there.'

'What about the bat? You hit her with a bat.'

Terry's eyes lit up a bit in horrified recall. 'Oh my God. Yeah. It was in the car. In the back seat. Must have belonged to one of her kids.'

'You don't remember that part, then?'

The sirens were definitely coming closer. He'd hear them soon. Jilly hoped they were for her.

'All I know is she was dead. I had to hide her. There were big garbage bins out along the street, the plastic things with the big wheels. Looked like trash pickup the next day. I carried her down the block. Had to work quick before I was seen. I took off her jewelry. She had her wallet with her 'cause I made her bring it. I figured I could dump her stuff around, someone would find it and it'd look like a robbery. Made sense. Druggie woman in a drug neighborhood. Served her right if people thought that of her.'

'You threw away the wallet. Someone found it. But why not her jewelry?'

'I was starting to toss stuff, trying to think straight. Didn't want to make it too obvious. Then some people started showing up. Dealers, I guess, like that. Bad sorts, the kind that come packing, you know? Some arguments and stuff started breaking out too. I got worried about being seen, being confronted for being where I shouldn't be. I took the jewelry back to the car with me.'

Bad sorts. Very possibly, Jilly thought, Marmaduke, who would shortly find the wallet.

She noted that as he got into trying to tell the story, his agitation subsided somewhat. She tried to keep him going. There was no telling what he was capable of, if that terrifying flash-fire anger was allowed to return. 'You hid the car,' she said, keeping her voice even. 'With everything still in it. You didn't get rid of it.'

'I was going to. Wasn't sure what to do. Everything was confused. Figured it'd be safe hidden away for now, while I got my head arranged. I couldn't remember ...'

Terry suddenly whipped his head around. Jilly figured he had heard the sirens and finally put two and two together. In the moment his attention was away, she steeled herself to spring for the bag. This might be it. She prepared to fight the giant man literally tooth and nail, if necessary.

But the sound that had distracted him was actually the closed front door being tried, followed by the sound of a key in the lock.

'Terry! What are you doing —'
'Melinda!'

She was holding a laundry basket, standing in the doorway, her mouth agape. She caught sight of Jilly on the floor.

'Detective Garvey!' She looked back and forth between them and dropped the basket. Her hand flew to her mouth. She had sized up the situation immediately.

'Melinda …' Terry turned toward her, stretching out a hand to her.

Jilly jumped for her bag. Terry spun around. For a big man he could move awfully fast.

'Terry!' screamed Melinda. 'No!'

'Time standing still' was a cliché Jilly had often heard, but she would later swear that it actually happened. She hurtled across the floor towards her bag, but it was clear that Terry was going to get in front of her and intercept her before she could reach it. It seemed to take forever. She kept repeating the same mantra in her head: she was smaller than the gigantic man reaching for her, but she was also not a terrified, frail woman like Jessica. She was a trained police officer. She might go down but she would not go easy. If she just said it enough, she might totally believe it.

Melinda's scream seemed to halt Terry in mid-air. He froze, unsure whether to continue to go after Jilly or to turn back to Melinda.

Jilly reached the bag, jamming her hand into it for her gun as she rolled over onto her back.

Terry was still bent towards Jilly but had turned his head back toward Melinda.

'Mrs. Pidgeon,' Melinda said, her voice breaking. 'You ... killed her? *You?*'

'Melinda, listen ...'

'You *killed* her!' Melinda yelled. 'You! What was done to her? How, Terry? How could you?'

'She was going to ruin your life,' Terry said pleadingly. 'Those people. They think they're better than us. So comfortable in their lives and so entitled. They have *everything*, and no idea of what it means to have to work for something! They don't care how hard you work ...'

'*Those people!*' Melinda shouted indignantly. 'I took care of *those people*! Those children — they did nothing, they're innocent, and now they don't have a mother! You took their *mother* away from them!'

'She was going to ruin everything! For you, for Olivia ...'

'She was a sick woman, Terry! She wasn't a bad person, she was confused! It would have worked out! I would have worked it out!'

'Melinda, I did it for you! For Olivia!'

Melinda's eyes widened hugely. She stared at him with amazed disbelief, then her face softened into sheer disappointment. 'No, Terry,' she whispered softly. 'You've done nothing for us. Nothing at all.'

The fight seemed to go out of him, just like that, and his shoulders drooped. He did not seem to notice that Jilly was now kneeling on one knee four feet behind him, grimly leveling her service automatic in a two-handed grip directly at his back, center mass, as per her police training.

The sirens were very loud now, and they were right outside Melinda's window. The wails died as several police cars screeched to a halt on the pavement, doors flew open, and a tumult of voices and urgent footsteps erupted.

Suddenly the apartment was flooded with uniformed officers, weapons drawn, barking orders. Jilly lowered her weapon and stood back to give them room, lowering her head and taking a deep breath. Amidst the chaotic ruckus, she could still clearly perceive the sound of Melinda Barstow's uncontrolled sobbing. Then she realized she could hear two voices crying. Terry Blaze, already being forcibly handcuffed by two officers, was weeping openly and loudly as well.

9

It was only a few minutes later that Dan arrived, and now only he, Jilly and Melinda remained in the apartment. Terry had been taken into custody and the din of the past half-hour was now replaced by a heavy stillness. Melinda sat at the edge of one of her armchairs, motionless, hands clasped in her lap, staring down at the ground. She had been that way since the officers had left with Terry. Jilly and Dan stood across the room, quietly conversing.

'I should have been with you,' Dan was repeating for the third time. It seemed to Jilly he was having a difficult time looking her in the eye. 'This is my fault. He could have killed you.'

'Dan, would you stop saying that? Nothing was your fault. We walk into bad situations all the time, it's part of the job.'

'But if I'd been with you ...'

'If you'd been with me, maybe it would've gone down differently, maybe not. But if

you hadn't called in the cavalry like that, maybe things would have been very different. Maybe Terry would be dead now.' *Or,* she thought without voicing, *not Terry but someone else.*

'As soon as I heard the hubbub on your end of the phone, I was out of there. Got on the horn for backup.'

'Got here pretty quick yourself. Hitchhike with a squad car?'

'Uh-huh. Pulled one over on the street, like in a movie.'

'So I guess this means you still didn't renew your license.'

Dan sighed. 'Least of my worries at the moment.'

Jilly walked over to Melinda, who did not look up. 'How are you doing?' she asked.

'Not well.'

'Do you need me to call your daughter or anyone?'

'Olivia is in class right now. She'll be home in a while. No need to let her know anything until then.'

'You might have saved my life, and Terry's as well, by coming in when you did. You do realize that, don't you? It was going

to be him or me.'

'I suppose, yes. I still can't believe he did this.' She looked up at Jilly with wide, red-rimmed eyes. 'I've known Terry for years. I would never have believed him capable of ... of what he did.'

Jilly said nothing. Melinda continued. 'I got that poor woman killed. I'm the cause of this horrible tragedy to her family.'

'No. Absolutely not. You can't let yourself think that way. This was nobody's fault but Terry's. What you said to him before was right. This could've somehow been worked out. Jessica was ill. She needed help. The problem was, nobody was in a position to help her, including you.'

'You're very good to tell me these things, Detective. But nothing will keep me from blaming myself for this. Not for a long time, perhaps.'

Jilly placed her hand on Melinda's shoulder. She knew Melinda was right and there was nothing more she could say.

$\star$ $\star$ $\star$

The service for Jessica Pidgeon was small, with only a handful in attendance, including her immediate family and Jilly and Dan. The serious-looking young man who stood beside Laurie, they decided, had to be her friend Robbie. She saw Melinda in the back of the church, far from the other mourners. Jilly noted that none of Jessica's friends had showed up, and most interestingly, neither had James's girlfriend Natasha. It was a melancholy finale to a case that had been unrelentingly depressing.

At the burial site, Jilly and Dan approached the family to offer their condolences. James thanked them for coming and introduced Jessica's mother. Jilly caught sight of Melinda making her way hastily from the gravesite. She had not stopped to talk to anyone.

Shortly thereafter, as they walked back to their cars, Jilly found the opportunity to walk a few steps away with Laurie. 'How are you holding up?' she asked the girl. She noted that Laurie had not visibly shed a tear through the service or the burial.

'I'm okay,' Laurie said. 'All things considered.'

'I hope you learn to forgive your mother. She was ...'

'Yeah, she was sick. Unhappy. I know. I keep hearing that.'

'She needed help but stopped asking for it. She loved you all deeply, even if she couldn't show it.'

Laurie looked down at the ground as she walked. 'My dad says he's coming home for good. I think he broke up with his lady friend. She's going to run his company when it's sold, or something like that. Anyway, he says he thinks he's needed more at home.'

'He's right.'

Laurie made a noise through her lips.

'Give him a chance, Laurie. Maybe he's learned something from all this. Please, will you try to do that?'

Laurie simply shrugged and said no more. They walked until they reached the short line of parked cars waiting to take them away from the cemetery. Jilly made her goodbyes and walked the few steps to her own car, where Dan was already waiting. This time, with a half-hearted smile, he got in behind the steering wheel. Jilly dropped herself onto the passenger seat with a deep sigh.

'Terry's arraignment is tomorrow,' Dan said as he started up the engine. 'Letitia and the rest of the newsies are announcing it all over the place. I wish I could say that's the end of it all.'

Jilly shook her head. 'Me too, partner.' She sat in thought for a while before continuing. 'Terry said that Jessica had everything, that she had no real problems. From his perspective it must've seemed that way. She had a beautiful home in a nice neighborhood, a comfortable life, a family. But none of it could save her from her own demons.'

Dan exhaled loudly. 'Great support system she had. Didn't seem like anybody close to her wanted to save her.'

'I wouldn't be too harsh on them, Dan. She didn't make it particularly easy for any of them. I keep thinking about what Brad told us about how depression pushes people away. That kid's wise beyond his years.'

'I was just thinking,' mused Dan. 'We always talk about how we're the ones who have to speak for the victim.'

'Uh-huh.'

'It seems Jessica had more people looking out for her after her death than she did while she was alive.'

'I'm afraid you're right, Dan.'

'They're all pretty damaged, aren't they? What do you think is going to become of all of them — the family, Melinda?'

'I have a feeling Melinda and Olivia will leave town and try to start over somewhere else, away from the notoriety of this case. She's a strong lady; she'll make the right choices. James is going to move back in with Brad and Laurie. Better late than never.'

She watched the cemetery pass by from the car window and searched for the hope in her heart. 'They'll find their way. Not tomorrow, but ultimately. It'll take a while, but they'll find their way.'

'Gotta believe.'

'Yeah.' Jilly nodded somberly.

That, she reflected, was sometimes all that kept her going. She had to keep believing.

We do hope that you have enjoyed reading this large print book.

Did you know that all of our titles are available for purchase?

We publish a wide range of high quality large print books including:
Romances, Mysteries, Classics
General Fiction
Non Fiction and Westerns

Special interest titles available in large print are:
The Little Oxford Dictionary
Music Book, Song Book
Hymn Book, Service Book

Also available from us courtesy of Oxford University Press:
Young Readers' Dictionary
(large print edition)
Young Readers' Thesaurus
(large print edition)

For further information or a free brochure, please contact us at:
Ulverscroft Large Print Books Ltd.,
The Green, Bradgate Road, Anstey,
Leicester, LE7 7FU, England.
Tel: (00 44) **0116 236 4325**
Fax: (00 44) **0116 234 0205**

Other titles in the
Linford Mystery Library:

THE EMERALD CAT KILLER

Richard A. Lupoff

A valuable cache of stolen comic books originally brought insurance investigator Hobart Lindsey and police officer Marvia Plum together. Their tumultuous relationship endured for seven years, then ended as Plum abandoned her career to return to the arms of an old flame, while Lindsey's duties carried him thousands of miles away. Now, after many years apart, the two are thrown together again by a series of crimes, beginning with the murder of an author of lurid private-eye paperback novels and the theft of his computer, containing his last unpublished book . . .